Mounta Love and Danger

by

Gail Pallotta

Acknowledgements

Cover picture - iStock Photos
Cover Designer - Vanessa Riley
Many thanks to Lisa Lickel for editing
To Mildred Colvin, Connie Almony,
Vanessa Riley and June Foster for encouragement
and recommendations
To my rock / mountain climbing friend
for his technical assistance
And to God for His many blessings

Chapter One - The Stranger in the Restaurant

The restaurant's panoramic view overlooking the clear, sparkling river in Fairwilde Kingdom nearly took away Gwendolyn Bante's breath. Purple mountain laurel, majestic hardwoods, and evergreen shrubs lined its banks like the finishing touches on a fine painting, but she sensed an eerie aura hanging over Derick's Down-Home Dining.

She picked up her tea glass as an enormous man with broad shoulders, long, muscular arms, and black stubble stormed in the door. He looked out of place in a white tee shirt as he plopped down at one of the linen-draped tables.

Uneasiness swept over Gwendolyn like an ill wind. "This place gives me the creeps. Why's there only one other customer?"

Jack Greenthumb started to turn around.

"No. Don't look at him," she said.

Jack relaxed in his seat.

"Why's the rough-looking guy in the tuxedo who showed us our table waiting on us? Don't they have any other employees?"

Jack rolled the captain's chair close to her. "More people will show up. It's a new restaurant, and it's beautiful. We're on the outskirts of Fairwilde."

"Is that the Awasi?" Gwendolyn leaned forward. "It looks like the same stream that runs by Greenthumb Acres and my house."

"Yes."

"I guess we can't be too far away, but the people aren't warm and friendly here. We might as well be on an alien planet."

The waiter strolled over and slapped down two paper menus so hard thuds resounded on the table, his hands coarse like those of someone who worked outdoors. He stared at Gwendolyn and Jack with cold blue eyes.

Jack pointed to an entree. "I'll have the prime rib. How about you, Gwenie? Does that sound good?"

"I guess."

Wrinkles creased the waiter's brow. "If you don't like prime rib, get something else." Harshness rattled in his low tone.

"No…that sounds delicious." Apprehension rumbled in Gwenie's gut. She leaned toward Jack when the waiter left. "I think we should leave."

"Nonsense, we just ordered. Soon everyone will be talking about this place, and we can tell them we've already been here." Jack gazed at Gwenie as though he could care less about the waiter's attitude.

The sun poured in the window glinting on his golden hair, making him look ironically angelic. "How did you hear about Derick's Down-home Dining?"

"Day before yesterday I was in town getting the initial car wax—"

"I should've known it had something to do with that red car. I saw you racing around in it." Gwenie wanted to add with Sue Herndon in a sarcastic tone, but Jack knew who he was with. Sue attracted guys like honey did bees. She had flowing blond hair, flirty blue eyes, and tight clothes that left little to the imagination.

"I was about to pay when this huge guy walks over and tells George Clark—you know, George, he owns the body shop."

"Yes, I know George."

"This big man comes in and tells him how good the food is at Derick's. Of course, I'm curious. Greenthumb Acres supplies fresh produce to all the restaurants in Fairwilde Kingdom, and I've never heard of Derick's." Jack raised his eyebrows. "Where's he getting his vegetables, and are they as great as this fellow says?"

Gwenie propped her elbow on the table and rested her hand on her fist. "So…this is a business lunch." Was Jack too pre-occupied professionally to see this place as it really was?

Jack nodded. "Yeah, partly." He put his hand on top of Gwenie's "But, I wanted you to experience this fine dining with me." Jack gazed at her with loving eyes. "I always want you with me when something's important."

The waiter served their food. He looked as out of place in his stiff white shirt as a rat standing at the table.

Jack cut into his entree and popped a bite in his mouth. "Hmm. That's good."

Gwenie tasted the green beans. "Down-home dining. Hmmph. Someone put these in the microwave." Her heart beat fast.

The large customer who'd come in earlier got up and wound around the tables and chairs toward them. Gwenie tapped Jack's leg with her foot.

His eyes snapped wide, and he whispered, "He's the one. He was at George's."

"Hullo." A shadow from the big fellow loomed over Gwenie's plate as he spoke in a gruff tone that put her on the edge of her seat.

"Hi." Jack's cheerful reply cut through the dark karma, but failed to keep Gwenie's knees from knocking under the table.

"You that Greenthumb kid?"

"Yes." The word came out of Jack's mouth in a questioning tone.

"I thought that wuz you listening the other day at the body shop when I told George how to get here."

Jack stuck out his hand. "Jack Greenthumb. Nice to meet you, ah—"

"You don't need to know who I am." The man's black eyes bored evil holes into Jack as he extended a large, wide hand with grease underneath the fingernails.

Terror held Gwenie to her seat like glue, or she would've gotten up and run.

"I talked to your old man the other day about Greenthumb Acres."

"Yes, sir. We sell produce to most of the restaurants in the area. I'm sure my father would add you to our list of clients."

The man knitted his brow. "My friends don't want to buy from him. They want to buy Greenthumb Acres."

Jack turned pale. "They what?"

"Want to buy it. My friends made him a fair offer, but he didn't agree. Why don't you go home and see if you can talk some sense into him?"

"Well, I don—"

Using all the strength Gwenie could muster, she kicked Jack under the table.

He jumped.

Words hung on the tip of her tongue. She breathed deep and swallowed. "Yes, Jack will do that. He'll explain the advantages of selling to his father."

The man's lips turned up on the corners into a sinister grin. "You got a bright lady friend. I'd keep her if I wuz you. What's your name?" He peered at Gwenie.

She dared not refuse to answer. Quick, a different name, not her real name. Nothing came to mind.

He slammed his hand on the table. "I *asked* you a question. No manners. I see."

"Gwendolyn. Gwendolyn Bante." A double-standard for sure. They couldn't know who he was, but he'd bullied her into giving him personal information.

"That's better. It was nice to meet you. You enjoy your lunch now."

Gwenie's insides turned to mush.

Sweat beaded on Jack's forehead as the man stomped away. He got out his wallet, pulled out the payment for their meal with a shaking hand, and laid it on the table. "Gwenie, let's go." Nervousness ran through his voice.

He got up, took Gwenie's arm, and guided her toward the door, whispering. "Walk natural. We'll be in the car soon."

"I hope the tires haven't been slashed."

Chapter Two - The Wreck

Gwenie charged from the plank front porch of the restaurant past decorative holly bushes onto the gravel lot, Jack beside her step for step. Sticky summer air nearly suffocated her as she flung the passenger door open with so much force it flew all the way back. She slid into the seat with horror running through her bones like electricity. "Let's get out of here."

Jack started the engine and raced up the steep, curvy road, the trees and underbrush a blur, the car bumping over ruts and rocks.

The rough drive jarred Gwenie's stomach. "I think we could slow down now before you wreck your new toy." *And I hurl.*

Jack decreased his speed a little.

"That's a restaurant open to the public? When we arrived, the empty parking lot gave me such a weird feeling I didn't notice whether or not there was a sign, but I looked back as we drove off. There isn't one—no name, no Derick's Down-Home Dining anywhere on the cabin. Think about it." Gwenie couldn't keep her voice from racing like her nerves.

"It's brand new. If it wasn't open for customers, why would that guy talk about it and give George directions? Why would they let us in and take our orders?"

Aggravation at Jack for his apparent lack of insight tingled over Gwenie's skin. "I don't know, but the way that brute threatened you, he sounded like a thug. Maybe it's some sort of hang-out for gamblers."

"I agree I didn't care for his tone of voice, and I wanted to get away from him, but I didn't see any gambling equipment or tables."

"They wouldn't put them out front when gambling's against the law in Fairwilde Kingdom. They're probably in the back. Does George gamble?"

"I don't know. He just waxed the car. We didn't share our life histories." An edge to Jack's voice told Gwenie he was irritated, but the color draining from his face let her know he paid attention to her concerns.

The cell phone lying on the black leather seat beside Jack rang. He glanced at it. "I have to pick up." He let go of the steering wheel with his right hand and grabbed it. "Hey Mom, what's up?"

The car swerved.

" Jack," Gwenie screamed.

Jack righted the vehicle. "I'm sorry, Mom." Silence. "Yes, I'll be careful and get there as soon as I can. I need to take Gwenie home." Stress lined Jack's voice.

Gwenie put her hand over her mouth. "What happened?"

"My dad's in the emergency room."

The car veered off the road onto the shoulder, sticks crunching underneath the tires.

"Are you all right?"

"I'm upset, but I'm okay." Jack steered the sporty vehicle back on course.

"What's wrong with your dad?"

"Someone beat him up."

"What!? Who would hurt a wonderful guy like your dad?" Had some dark force taken over Fairwilde?

Jack's head wobbled. "Gwenie, I'm not feeling so good."

***

Jack forced open his heavy-as-lead eyelids, his face in a deflated airbag. He peered at the leaves of a large oak tree covering his cracked windshield. "Gwenie." He turned in her direction and choked on his breath.

She was slumped forward. Her head lay on the dashboard. Why hadn't they put on their seatbelts? A sinking sensation coursed through Jack's bones. They'd been in too big a hurry to get away from Derick's Down-Home Dining. What had he done?

Gwenie wasn't moving. He touched her arm as tears pooled in his eyes. "Oh, please wake up!" He rolled down the window, sucked in air, and shook his head until the fog in it dissipated.

Gwenie just hadn't come to yet. She was all right. She had to be. He placed his fingers on her wrist---a weak pulse. His chest tightened as he punched the ignition button and shoved the car in reverse. "Hang in there, Gwenie. I'll get you to the hospital."

Still as a statue, she never flinched.

The car's wheels spun. "Oh, please, dear God, help me move from this God-forsaken place." Jack floor-boarded the pedal. The engine roared. The tires whirred, but the car didn't move. He didn't want to wait for a wrecker, but he had no choice.

He snatched up the cell phone and turned it on. The blank screen taunted him. He shook the useless piece of junk and mashed the on button again and again. He threw it on the floorboard.

Gwenie's little black pocketbook lay beside her. He grabbed it and yanked out her phone, punching the on button—nothing. His finger mashed it over and over. Help wasn't coming. Hope fell from him like bricks tumbling from a wall.

He grabbed the driver's door handle and pushed, but it stayed shut. He shoved harder.as alarm charged through him like electricity. He scooted over and shoved his entire body at the door. It flew open, and he fell face down onto leaves and underbrush. Blood oozed down his cheek as he got up. He wiped it with his handkerchief and stepped to the front of the car.

Big tree limbs lodged in the front bumper holding it prisoner. He tried to lift one, but it barely budged. He surveyed the mountainside of thick trees and underbrush then headed toward the dirt road, keeping his eyes focused on the ground until he spotted a strong branch he could use for leverage. He had to get Gwenie out of there.

A motor rattled in the distance. A big black truck headed toward him, dust and rocks spraying from its tires. Who was it? Was the driver going to hit him? Jack jumped to the side and tried to rub the fog from his head. The rattling stopped. A door slammed. Footfalls crunched in the leaves growing louder with each step. If the pounding in his brain would only settle down so he could think.

A pair of brown military boots stood in front of him. He let his eyes wander up huge blue-jeaned legs to a white tee shirt stretched across a broad chest. He lifted his head and peered at the man's face. His heart fell to his stomach.

"What've you done, squirt?"

Jack's voice caught on the knot in his throat, the lush green forest closing in on him, the stirred-up dust drying his mouth.

"I'm a neighborly sort. I'll help you out." A smug grin spread across the intimidator, the only other customer who'd been in the restaurant.

Jack didn't want anything to do with him, but he had to get Gwenie to a hospital.

"Ah, don't worry. I ain't gonna' hurt ya." The guy meandered to the passenger's side of the car. "Looks like the smart lady friend's in a bad way—bad to the gut."

Bad to the gut. What was he talking about?

"Almost looks like a mannequin with all that auburn hair spread out on the dashboard."

Sick.

The burly man stomped around to the front of the car. "Here's the problem. Oh, I see. That's why you're holding that stick. You were gonna' wedge it in between the bumper and these limbs. I don't think I'll need it." He wrapped his huge hands around the offending branches, squatted down, snorted, grunted, and stood, pulling them off the bumper, uprooting the tree. He brushed off his hands. "There ya' go. Get the lady to the hospital."

Relief rippled all over Jack in spite of his disdain for the brute. He reached for his wallet. "How much do I owe you?"

"You don't owe me nothin'. Just deliver the message I gave you to your father."

Jack's stomach churned, and he gagged. "Oh, I think he got your message loud and clear. That's why I was in such a rush to get to the hospital."

"Don't waste time with her hurt. Just tell him what I said."

He was right about not hanging around to argue. "All right." Whose delivery man was this guy? What shape was Dad in?

"I'll back up and wait to make sure you get that thing out."

His offer sent anxiety racing up Jack's spine. "Thank you." He spoke over his shoulder, even though he wanted to get away from the burly man.

Jack opened the creaking, damaged door, charged into the front seat, and started the engine. Uncertainty gripped him as he shoved the wrecked car in reverse with a shaking hand. It moved backward. *Thank you, Lord.* Now if it would keep running until he could get help for Gwenie.

The truck followed him to the end of the dirt road. Jack turned left toward Fairwilde General Hospital, and the huge man went right.

Jack peered over a bashed-in hood. His new sports car looked like it'd been in a demolition derby, but he couldn't have cared less. All the way to the emergency room worry for the life of his father and Gwenie shook his insides. He prayed, "Oh, dear Lord, please let them be all right."

Finally, Fairwilde General appeared in the distance, ambulances passing Jack as he turned onto the road leading to the hospital. He glanced at Gwenie. Tears welled up inside him. He swallowed to keep them from overflowing as he pulled into the lot at ER and parked. People in green scrubs and blue uniforms passed in and out the doorway, hurrying to and from ambulances and everyday vehicles.

Jack sprang out of the car. "Can someone help me, please?"

Two paramedics rushed over, a stocky red-haired man and a woman with long, curly blond hair.

"Sure, buddy. What's wrong?" Redhead asked.

Words stuck in Jack's throat as he pointed to Gwendolyn.

The blond spoke into a mouthpiece. "Get a stretcher out here stat."

Redhead flung open the passenger door. Hovering over Gwenie, he leaned her back and applied an oxygen mask from a black bag he'd set beside him. Then he placed his fingers atop her wrist.

"She has a pulse." Faint hope flickered inside Jack as he spoke the words.

The red-headed guy nodded. "Yeah, buddy. We'll take good care of her." Sympathy glinted in his blue eyes. "What's her name?"

"Gwendolyn Bante."

"Does she have any conditions we should know about? Allergies?"

Jack had never heard Gwenie mention anything. "I don't think so."

Two orderlies came out with a stretcher and carefully lifted Gwenie onto it.

A pain pierced Jack's heart like a sword as he trailed behind them. She had to be all right. He'd hate himself for the rest of his life if Gwenie were hurt badly, or worse yet----

He couldn't think it.

The red-headed paramedic tapped him on the shoulder. "Sorry, buddy. We need to get you checked out, have you fill out some papers, and make an official police report. Let the doctors do their job. I'll make sure you see her later." He offered a handshake. "I'm Ted Davis, by the way." Gentleness penetrated his busy, business-like voice.

"Jack Greenthumb."

"I see you have a small cut on your cheek. It doesn't need stitches. I'll clean it and put a Band-Aid on it for you."

Jack touched his face. "Oh yeah. It's nothing, but sure, it's probably best to take care of it."

Ted smiled and reached in his bag as the yearning to go with Gwenie filled every part of Jack. But he knew Ted was right.

Chapter Three - The Shadow

Gwenie touched the top of her head. Had someone dropped a pile of bricks on it? She moved it the tiniest bit. "Ouch" A sinking sensation swept through her. Something was very wrong.

She opened her eyes. White all around. Where was she? She blinked several times and a door came into focus. But a door to where? She spread out her arm to feel the space around her, but quickly pulled it back as a sharp pain shot through her skull.

A shadow moved toward her. "Miss Bante." Someone in the distance called out to her. "Miss Bante."

Deep inside Gwenie formed the word "Yes." It sounded weak to her ears, but she heard it. If she weren't so drained, she'd be afraid, but she didn't have the energy.

"Good. You're awake. You've had a nasty bump. The paramedics believe you've had a concussion, so we want you to lie quietly. I'm Sue Ellen Sprant. Your friend gave me your purse, and I put it right here." She pulled open the drawer in the nightstand and pointed.

Gwenie nodded, and it hurt.

"I'll return to check on you and bring you a hospital gown, but if you need anything press this button."

Sue Ellen handed Gwenie a small black handle.

She took it and ran her finger over a bump on the top. That must be the button. She breathed deep and let the air out slowly as Sue Ellen moved away. Then she reached in the drawer and took out her purse, clutching it to her chest. Jack would call soon. She rummaged in her pocketbook until she located her cell phone and stuck it in her bra where she could get to it in a flash. She didn't want a hospital gown, but Jack would probably be here before the shadow brought one back.

She closed her eyes. A concussion. No wonder her head ached. An image of speeding in Jack's red car up a dirt road flashed in her mind. They'd been to that new restaurant he'd heard about that really wasn't a restaurant. She'd been scared out of her wits. Toward the end of the meal when this big—no huge—guy with black stubble gave Jack a message about buying Greenthumb Acres, Jack got frightened too. She'd seen it in his face.

Why wasn't Jack here? He might drive other girls around in his spiffy red car, but when she needed him, he was always around. It'd been that way since first grade when he'd pulled her pigtails, but wouldn't let anyone else yank them. Tears welled up and spilled onto Gwendolyn's eyelashes. She had to get out of this white room and find Jack.

A creak broke the silence. She didn't see Sue Ellen and she hadn't mashed the button. Where was the button? She must have dropped it. But Sue Ellen would give it back to her when she checked on her. The steps grew louder. The footfalls sounded like thunder. Sue Ellen walked softly like a shadow and made no noise.

Chapter Four - Detained at the Hospital

Jack finished filling out the papers and rubbed his aching head while he waited in a chair in the hall outside the ER with Ted. His nerves raced like a revved up engine while the ambulance drivers, nurses, and patients going back and forth blurred into the background. He searched for a way to escape to go find Gwenie and his dad.

"Let's get you settled." Ted guided Jack to a large antiseptic room with nine patients. Pulling on a curtain attached to a rod at the top of a bed, Ted gestured toward it. "I gotta' run, but Dr. Ames will be right here."

"I just want to see—"

"Gwendolyn. I know. It won't be long."

Ted exited through a slit in the drape, and Jack sat down.

He could flee through the opening, but with the luck he'd had today he'd run into Ted. He'd make him come back and the whole process would take even longer.

Dr. Ames slipped in and extended his meticulously clean hand.

"I understand you received a bump on the head in a car accident." The tall, slender doctor studied his clipboard with intense blue eyes. He pulled a small light out of his jacket pocket and checked Jack's pupils. "Hmm. Good. Follow my finger with your eyes."

Dr. Ames moved his digit right, left, up and down. "Do you have a headache?"

"Not bad." Maybe if he didn't complain about any ailments he'd let him go.

"Where'd you hit your head?"

"I have a knot here." Jack touched a spot near the middle of his forehead.

Dr. Ames felt of it. "Better swelling outside than in. Stand up and hop on one foot."

Jack slid his feet to the floor and lifted his right leg. Silent screams to get out of here and find Gwenie echoed in his brain as he performed a quick, soft jump.

"Good."

"Can I go now?"

"I believe you're fine, but I can't let you leave until a nurse checks your vital signs and takes you for a CT scan."

Aggravation tingled all over Jack. "What's that?"

"Technically it's cranial computed tomography. In your case, hopefully it will rule out a concussion. Just lie down and relax, someone will be along soon. I'll come back and officially release you."

He must be kidding. Did Dr. Ames really think he could relax with every nerve in his body on edge because he wanted to get out of here?

An orderly entered, helped Jack onto a gurney, and whisked him to Imaging Services.

A blond-haired woman with a nice figure in a blue uniform stood beside a scanner above a narrow examining table. She patted it. "Hi, can you get up here for me?"

"Sure." Jack did as she asked, but he was going to pop out of his skin if he didn't leave soon.

"I want you to lie perfectly still while the scan runs. I'll be in the next room, and I may need you to hold your breath from time to time."

"Okay." If he ever wanted to get something right the first time he did now.

The technician left and apparently turned on the machine. He slid under the CT scanner and lay as still as stone. She said, "Okay, hold your breath."

He did and the apparatus clicked. She repeated the action a few times, dragging out the word hold. Then finally she finished.

An orderly returned and rolled him to his bed in the large antiseptic room. "Okay, buddy, Dr. Ames will be back soon. In the meantime, Captain Jones will be in to ask you a few questions.

"Captain Jones?!"

"Yeah, from the police department. They need an accident report."

Jack's blood boiled as the orderly left the room. This morning he was free as a bird riding around in his new red car. He put his head in his hands. Surely they didn't expect him to talk to a policeman before he saw Gwenie and Dad. Gwenie. She had to be okay. Soon it would be like nothing ever happened. They'd laugh together, even eat lunch and talk about the crazy waiter.at Derrick's Down-Home Dining or whatever that place was. Why was this taking so long? Jack fidgeted as a wave of fear swept over him. For the first time he wondered if he would ever see Gwenie again.

Chapter Five - Gwenie's Capture

Flat on her back, Gwenie stared at the ceiling. The white hospital room seemed to vibrate with heavy footfalls. It couldn't be Sue Ellen. She walked too softly. Gwenie lifted her head.

A large hand with dark hair on the knuckles that rubbed against her nose slapped a cloth over her mouth.

Her head swung back. "Wait. Stop. I can't breathe. Mmmm." Flailing, she thrust her arms outward like a defensive lineman trying to hold off an opposing player, but the smell overtook her.

Black.

***

Gwendolyn floated in darkness until something cold hit her in the face.

"Help. Help," she screamed as loud as she could.

The burly man from Derick's Down-Home Dining threw ice water at her.

"You're all right Sweet Cakes. They'll come for you, and take you back to the squirt as soon as his old man sells Greenthumb Acres."

The man's round mouth with small, yellowed teeth came into focus.

"Who are you? Who are they? Where am I?"

"Now, I ain't dumb. I'm not gonna tell you."

"I'm supposed to rest. I have a concussion. Do you want my demise or brain damage on your conscience?"

The huge burly man's lips drew to a straight line. Shock filled his angry, wide eyes. "No ma'am, I'm not a murderer."

Anger seethed like hot coals in Gwenie's stomach. "You just kidnap people?"

"Don't get smart with me." The man with bitumen eyes guffawed.

Gwenie fought tears with all her might. She would not cry in front of this brute.

"I see that bottom lip trembling. No need to be afraid. All you have to do is lay low until the deal's done. You can recover from your concussion on the sofa right here in the den. We have a television."

Gwenie gazed around. The gray plank walls resembled the unfinished cedar boards on the deck on the back of their house, but she was indoors. There was a floor-to-ceiling window on the right. The TV Burly Man mentioned sat on a black metal stand in front of her.

She craned her neck to see out the window. Nothing but foliage, but Jack could climb up anything. If she stayed here, he'd easily spot her when he came to get her. Just like hide and seek when they were kids. He always found her. "I'd like to be anywhere but here."

"I'm warning you. I can't stand smart-alecks." The monster drew back his hand.

Gwenie put her arms over her head.

"Grrrr." Burly man pounded the palm of his right hand with his other fist so hard an eerie echo hung in the air.

Gwenie straightened up, her head swimming. *Jack, please hurry.* Fright exploded inside her like firecrackers. "Could I rest here, please?" Her gaze fell to the magazines on the coffee table. Her head hurt too bad to read, but she had to calm down the burly man. I'd like to look at some of those, or maybe a book from the bookcase. What titles do you have?"

"That's more like it. No reason we can't be friends. I ain't much of a reader, but I'll turn the TV on for you." He punched the green button on a remote and handed it to her.

"What's your name?" She asked as she took it.

"I told you at the restaurant. You don't need to know who I am."

"Okay, but what am I supposed to call you if I'm going to be in the same house with you?"

"Noble."

Gwenie tried not to grimace when she heard the word. How could she call such a monster Noble. She had to. "All right, Noble it is."

What else would she have to do to survive?

Chapter Six - Captain Jones

Jack rubbed the loosely woven white spread. It had sixty threads covering the area where he sat. One, two, three, four...the drape had seventy-five fine gray lines barely visible. One, two, three, four...the floor around the bed on one side had sixteen square beige tiles. Aggravation crawled all over his skin. Where was Captain Jones?

A lanky blond-haired policeman entered through the slit. "Hi, I'm Carl Jones, Fairwilde Police."

Jack extended his hand and they shook.

"How you feeling?"

"I'm fine. Let's take care of this."

The policeman whipped a pad out of his pocket. "Okay, what happened?"

"I hit a tree."

Captain Jones nodded. "Any other vehicles involved?" His voice sounded matter-of-fact.

"No."

"Where were you?"

"On a dirt road off the thoroughfare that starts at the bottom of the mountain and goes to the top. That's Highway 191, right?" Jack trembled inside for wanting to charge out and find Gwenie.

"Correct. Does this dirt road have a name?"

"I didn't see one."

"Why were you on it?"

"I'd taken Gwenie—" Jack's voice cracked—" to eat at Derick's Down-Home Dining."

Captain Jones scratched his chin. "I've never heard of it. I thought I'd eaten in every restaurant in Fairwilde Kingdom. Guess not."

Jack's heart sank as an image of the isolated, deserted building flashed in his mind. Maybe it wasn't legitimate. "It's new." How could something so simple as taking his girlfriend to lunch turn into such a disaster? He had to get out of here and find her.

"All right. Tell me about Derick's and the crash."

Jack touched his lips with his fingertips. "The dirt road dead ends at the bottom of the incline in a parking lot in front of a log cabin. That's Derrick's. It's by the river."

"You were leaving the restaurant when you wrecked, right?"

"Yes sir. I was on the way here to see my dad."

Captain Jones scratched his head. "What's wrong with your father?"

Jack's heart rate accelerated. "I'm not sure yet." He hoped Captain Jones heard the impatience in his tone and would let him go.

Captain Jones nodded, but no such luck. "How fast were you going?"

"I'd say fifty or fifty-five."

Captain Jones's mouth gaped. "On a dirt road? What was the hurry?"

"I needed to get Gwenie out of there and get her home. Now I don't even know where she is. I need to find her if she's even----." He'd tried to emphasize the word "need" so Captain Jones would dismiss him, but his voice shook.

"They'll take good care of your girlfriend here. What happened next?"

"I don't know. I was rushing to get to the hospital. I got dizzy right before I banged into the tree, and I must have been knocked out on impact."

Captain Jones shifted his weight. "I see. When you came to, you left and brought Miss Bante here, right?"

"After the guy from the restaurant got the tree branches off the car bumper."

Captain Jones's eyes snapped wide. "There was a witness?"

"No. He came along after we crashed and stopped to help."

"Did you get his name?" Urgency lined Captain Jones's voice as though he needed more information about the burly man.

"I'm sorry. I don't know."

Captain Jones rubbed his chin. "Odd that he didn't call to report the accident and ask for an ambulance." He spoke in a softer tone as though he was assessing something and not sharing all of his thoughts.

Was the big burly guy a gangster like Gwenie thought? A shiver snaked up Jack's spine.

Captain Jones flipped his pad shut and put away his pen. "Can you describe him?"

"He's the biggest man I've ever seen, and he has—" Jack almost said evil-looking eyes. He swallowed. "He has eyes that look black. They match his dark hair and the stubble on his face."

"How tall? What about his weight?"

"It's hard to say. I'd guess at four hundred pounds and seven feet five inches tall."

Captain Jones's eyebrows shot up. "He is big. Okay, thanks."

"Can I leave now to go see my girlfriend and my dad?"

"As soon as Dr. Ames releases you. It shouldn't be much longer." He held a card out to Jack. "If you think of anything else, call."

Jack took it and stuck it in his shirt pocket. "Yes, sir."

Jack had done everything they'd asked from filing the police report to hopping around for the doc to lying like a mummy for the scan. Enough.

He got up to leave, but the room spun. He lay down. There was nothing wrong with him when they brought him to this ER cubicle, and there was nothing wrong now except his heart pounded against his chest like a drum for wanting to hear his dad's voice and wrap Gwenie in his arms. He couldn't wait to tell her he never wanted to ride anyone but her around in his red car. He'd loved her since the first grade, and he still loved her with all his heart. Not knowing what was wrong with her made his insides roar like a caged tiger.

The split in the curtain opened and Dr. Ames entered. He studied his chart. "Well, it looks like we can give you the okay to leave if you feel like it." He shifted his gaze to Jack. "You're so pale. Maybe, you better rest a while longer."

"No."

The doctor cringed.

Jack hadn't meant to have such loud rebellion in his voice. "Sorry. I'll be fine if I can get out of here and find Gwendolyn Bante and my father. I was on my way to see my dad when we wrecked."

Dr. Ames bit his bottom lip. "I understand."

"Good." Jack swung his legs over the side of the bed and the room swirled. He didn't dare let Dr. Ames know. He sat down and peered as attentively as he could at Dr. Ames as though he waited for his instructions.

"An orderly will be along to take you out."

"I'm only going to the lobby."

Dr. Ames smiled. "It's hospital policy. He'll roll you there."

"How much longer?" Jack wanted to scream, but these people would have their way no matter what.

"He'll be right here." Dr. Ames handed Jack his discharge papers. Then he left.

Jack breathed deep, a freeing sensation running through him. Soon he'd be on his way. He didn't want to admit it, but they were right. Relief that he checked out just fine relaxed his tight muscles and having the accident on record gave him reassurance.

A wheelchair rolled into the cubicle. Then the stocky guy with dark hair pushing it appeared. "Dr. Ames says we need to get you out of here." His cheerful, bubbly voice filled the air as he twirled the chair around and stopped in front of Jack.

Jack stood, and the orderly reached out to steady him. Good thing. Jack saw two of him, but it was because anxiety over Gwenie and Dad ran over his nerves like a wire dish scrubber. He'd be fine once he saw them.

Chapter Seven - Looking for Dad and Gwenie

Jack walked down the hall, his heart thumping, the smells of antiseptics and sickness gagging him. He hurried by some rooms with shut doors and others with lifeless-looking forms lying between white sheets in beds with iron sides. Finally, he reached the main lobby.

A lady with long orange fingernails pecked at a computer at the receptionist's desk. She looked up and gazed at him with kind hazel eyes, the only brightness in this sad room of black easy chairs and matching sofas. "How may I help you?"

"I'm looking for Fred Greenthumb and Gwendolyn Bante."

"And, who are you?"

"I'm Jack Greenthumb. Fred's my father, and Gwendolyn's my girlfriend."

The woman checked her computer. "Mr. Greenthumb is in room 101. Ms. Bante's on the third floor in 341." She smiled as though she wished she could bring sunshine into the gloom hanging over him.

"Thank you." Stretched in two directions like a rubber band that could snap at any instant, Jack stepped toward the elevator to take it to 341 to see Gwenie, but then he turned and headed down the hall toward Dad's room. No wait. He pivoted and marched to the elevator again. Only seconds to Dad. He did an about face and practically ran to 101.

He stopped short at the door. With Dad's salt-and-pepper-colored hair slicked back from his face, and his head lying on the white pillow, he looked like Jack's grandfather had in his casket. A head rush hit Jack, and he grabbed the doorjamb.

Jack's mom, Melisse, sat in a black, vinyl chair in the corner by the window with her head lowered.

Jack pulled back his shoulders, willing himself to be strong for both of them even though his body had turned to mush. Gwenie would tell him to pray. Gwenie. Tears built inside him as he remembered her lying with her head on the dashboard of the red car.

Dear Lord, give me courage as I try to help Mom, Dad, and Gwenie.

He forced himself to take another step.

Mom looked up, sadness swimming in her blue eyes, and her lips turned down. "She sprang from her seat and hugged Jack so tight she squeezed some of the strength that came from her faith into him.

"Look at him. He has a black eye, a cracked rib and a broken arm. He's such a gentle—" Mom put her small hands over her face as tears ran down her cheeks.

Swelling puffed around Dad's eye on the right side.

A knot formed in Jack's throat, but he swallowed his sorrow. "I'm so grateful he isn't hurt worse. God must have been looking after him." The words came from Jack's soul, an answer to his prayer he believed.

All of them went to church and prayed, but Dad always had said it was better to show people God's love by the way you lived—and he did. He didn't deserve this. Who would beat him up? And why?

Oh no, the message. Jack put his hand over his mouth. Was the entire visit to the restaurant a set-up? Had the burly guy talked about it in town so Jack would hear him? That was a bit far-fetched. Other people would've heard it too. But the place had been deserted. What a fool he'd been. He gazed at Dad's
swollen face. How could he mention a threat with him in that shape?

Dad held out his left arm, the one without the cast, and Mom sat down.

"Hello son." Dad squinted his good eye. "Did you cut yourself shaving?"

Jack touched his cheek. "Oh, it's just a little nick. How do you feel?"

Dad moved his head as though he meant to shake it. "Probably not as bad as I could, but I need to get out of here and get back to the farm. There are jobs to oversee at the factory and in the green houses."

Dad had worked so hard not only for his own good, but for that of Fairwilde. He'd come here from Ireland as Fred O'Cattie and settled at the base of these mountains where apple trees, and not much else, grew plentifully. Dad planted those along with potatoes, squash, green beans, every vegetable imaginable, and to the surprise of his neighbors, they all had flourished. So many people started calling him Fred Greenthumb he officially changed his name.

It had been so like his dad to expand his fields and share his crops with those who had little to eat. To give him something in return, they helped erect his processing plant, or factory as he called it. He employed over one hundred of them, and they started paying for the produce they needed.

Everyone loved his dad. Who did this? "Dad, just tell me what you need. I'll handle it."

Dad patted Jack's hand with his good one. "I don't want a single employee to miss his or her payment. If you could get out the checks—"

"Of course I will."

"Thank you, son."

Jack needed to tell his Dad what the burly man had said. Clearly someone had already sent a message to the entire family. His dad looked so helpless. Maybe he'd wait and not mention the restaurant fiasco until Dad got out of the hospital. "How long do they want to keep you?"

"They haven't said, but surely in a day or so I can manage the books, and you or Melisse can write the checks."

"Oh no, Dad, I'll handle the payroll and let Mom take care of you. It's not that." Jack lowered his head.

"Well what is it?"

Jack looked up and met his dad's eyes, a questioning look in the good one not nearly shut from swelling. The words stuck in Jack's throat.

"Son, what's wrong? Whatever it is, I need to know." Dad tried to rise up.

"No Fred, be still." Mom's voice sounded shrill as it usually did when she was anxious. She hopped up from her chair.

Dad lay back on his pillow.

Mom and Dad stared at Jack with intense eyes as though they were at his mercy for information.

Jack brushed his hair off his forehead. Where to begin? "I overheard a man in town talking about a new restaurant."

"Yes." His mother gave him her out-with-it look.

"I picked up Gwenie, and we went there. After we finished eating this huge, burly-looking guy came over to the table—" He couldn't say it. He couldn't blurt out what happened to Gwenie and him. Knowing about the wreck was the last thing they needed. They'd find out soon enough when they went home and saw the car.

Mom put her hand on her hip.

"He wanted me to give Dad a message."

"For the love of all that's good, tell us." Aggravation laced Mom's voice.

"He said for Dad to sell the farm to the people who asked to buy it." Jack directed his gaze at his dad. "From the sound of his voice, I took it as a threat. Has anyone contacted you?"

"I got a call last week from a man insisting I sell all the property I owned, but I told him I wasn't interested. He said I'd hear from him." Dad touched his swollen face with his left hand. "Apparently, I have."

Fury raced up Jack's spine. "What's his name?"

"He wouldn't tell me. He said he was just representing the buyer. All I had to do was agree to sell, and his lawyers would handle everything."

"The burly guy wouldn't give me his name either. Who could he be? And what do these people want with the farm?"

Dad raised his head off the pillow. "I don't know. We left right after the attack, and your mother called the police as soon as we got here. The police came to my room to get a report. I didn't mention the call I received about selling the property to them because I didn't connect the two." Dad's voice sounded angry, but strained from weakness. "I should contact the authorities now and let them know."

Jack balled his hands into fists, flexed them then motioned for his dad to lie back. "Just rest. I'll take care of it. Where were you when the attack occurred?"

"I was headed to the factory to talk to Bob Casey, my new manager. Two men wearing black ski masks flew out from behind the Red Tipped Photinias growing beside it and got the jump on me. That's all I remember until I came to. Then they were gone."

Jack scratched his head. "Why would they do all of this just to make you sell the farm?"

Dad sighed. "Son, I can't imagine. It's not like there's a gold mine on it."

Jack nodded. "Right. I need to go now and take care of a few things. You rest and get well."

He stepped into the hall and met their maid, Bertille, and Fernando Flourez, the hot house manager. Apparently, they had come all the way into town to visit his dad. Bertille hugged him. "Don't you fret, Mister Jack. I'll take good care of your daddy."

"Thank you."

Bertille had started working for Jack's grandfather twenty years ago when Dad was learning the business. He thought of her as part of the family, and Mom claimed Bertille as one of her best friends. From Bertille's sniffing and wiping her eyes, Jack would say the feeling was mutual.

Fernando patted Jack on the back. "I'll make sure the hot houses and the fields run as smoothly as possible."

Fernando had worked in the green houses ever since Dad had built them. A gentle man, he'd come to Fairwilde from the Spanish Kingdom and appeared to have brought a love of flowers with him. He seemed to have the right touch to make even the delicate orchids flourish.

Jack shook his hand. "I know you will."

He rushed down the corridor. When he cleared hearing distance of Dad's room, he pulled out Captain Jones's card and punched the number into his cell phone. "Hi, this is Jack Greenthumb. My dad's in room 101 on the main floor at the hospital. He's here because he was beaten up by thugs. My mom called to report the attack. Dad's been questioned, but what he didn't tell the policemen is this. Before he was assaulted an unknown caller tried to convince him to sell the farm. Dad told him no."

"Did he know his attacker?"

"No. there were two of them wearing black ski masks." Jack choked up.

Chapter Eight - Nurse Pain in My Side

Jack's insides shook like a building with bricks falling one by one as he marched to the elevator. He hit the up button and waited while his stomach rolled like a hay baler. How many days did it take to get a ride upstairs?

He pivoted, rushed through the lobby, and flung open the door to the gray stairwell. Dust scattered as he stepped on the cement landing spurred on by worry pulsing through his veins. Taking two stairs at a time he ran to the third floor and charged through the doorway to the nurses' station. Gasping for breath, he placed his hands on his knees. "Gwendolyn Bante, room 341, which way?"

The RN in a navy blue uniform peered over blue-rimmed spectacles. "It's on the right. You look as though you could use a glass of water."

"I'm okay." Jack spun around. "No time for it," he spoke over his shoulder as he nearly broke into a run. *Gwenie. Gwenie. I'm coming.* He bounded into the room.

The thin, blue cotton spread lay crumpled at the end of the bed, the sheets wrinkled. Jack put his ear to the closed bathroom door, listening for a couple minutes. He knocked. "Gwenie. It's me. Are you all right?" He tapped harder. Still no answer.

Fear hit him in the gut as he walked back to the nurses' station.

"Yes, may I help you?" She spoke soft expressionless words while Jack wanted to yell.

"Gwenie. Gwendolyn Bante's gone."

The lady of mercy waved her small, thin hand. "Someone's probably taken her to have a test. Why don't you have a seat in the waiting area and relax?"

Jack bolted. "Excuse me, are you listening, Miss-uh?" Jack glanced at her nametag. "Miss Charms."

"Yes, you're trying to tell me that Miss Bante has left the hospital, and I can see as plain as day on my computer screen. She's in room 341."

"No she's not." Sweat beaded on Jack's forehead.

"Perhaps she isn't there literally right now." Aggravation flashed in Miss Charms' eyes. "As I just explained, patients do leave their rooms temporarily."

"Why don't you come look?"

"I believe you. I'll not leave my station until the floor nurses return from their rounds. Miss Bante will appear shortly. Why don't you—"

"Get me security." Jack roared like thunder.

"Sir, you need to sit down." Miss Charms turned prune-faced. "I'll get security all right." She picked up the receiver on the desk.

Jack strolled to the empty third-floor lobby, plopped down in a black vinyl chair beside a water cooler, and tapped his foot on the gray laminate floor to keep from jumping out of his skin. *You'll see, Nurse Pain in My Side.*

A pudgy guy dressed in a navy uniform and black shoes with worn soles on the sides waddled to Jack. His nametag read Ray Bertz. "I hear you've been aggravating Miss Charms."

Jack shot out of his chair. "I've been trying to tell her Gwendolyn Bante, the girl who's supposed to be in 341, is missing."

The wrinkles in the security guard's brow eased. "All right, let's go see."

He strolled with Jack to Gwenie's room.

Jack motioned toward the empty bed, the sun shining in the window highlighting a wide stripe across the middle of the rumpled covers.

Ray glanced at it then at Jack. "She's probably in the bathroom."

"Be my guest." Jack swung his arm in that direction.

Ray tapped. Nothing. He knocked again. "Ma'am, ma'am, are you in there?"

He pushed on the door. "It's either stuck or locked." He shoved harder and it flew open. There was no one in the room. "Hmm. All right, I'll have

Miss Charms get a couple orderlies to check this hall. If she doesn't turn up—"

Jack glared at him. "Call the cops and put out an APB."

"Sometimes patients get confused, wander around, and end up in the wrong place. I'm looking into it. Be patient."

Jack walked with the guard to the nurse's station, where three other ladies in navy blue uniforms gathered around Miss Charms.

"Yes?" Her expressionless voice floated up.

"He's right. Miss Bante's not in 341. Get a couple guys up here to check for her."

"I know she isn't in there, but patients leave their rooms all the time for tests."

The security guard pointed at the charts on the desk. "Wouldn't one of those tell you if she were having one?"

Miss Charms looked through them and opened one. She looked down and mumbled, "She did have a head injury." She peered up. "We'll look in every room, closet, and corner on this hall. If we don't find her, we'll call you." Strain lined her voice.

The security guard glared at her. "You should have already checked for her."

She waved her hand. "You try doing this job."

The security guard turned to Jack. "I don't think she's going to have that position much longer." He mumbled as he motioned toward the lobby.

Jack's nerves exploded like a bomb. "How long will the search take?"

"Have a seat—"

"This is ridiculous. She's gone." Jack's loud growl echoed down the hall.

Chapter Nine - Danger

Jack charged liked a bull out the doorway of the emergency room into the hot summer day past two ambulances and a police car. Three people in street clothes headed toward him as he ran between a yellow sedan and a black truck in the crowded parking lot to the banged-up vehicle.

Would it get him to Gwenie? It had to. The door squeaking as he flung it back didn't slow him a bit. He got in and burned rubber. Which way should he go? Where should he look? He shook his head to clear it, his pulse pounding in his temples as he sped down Main Street in Fairwilde Village.

The police station came into view. The last thing he needed—to be stopped by the police. His brakes squealed as he slammed them, but he slowed in time to drive the speed limit by the red brick building.

Gwenie loved the ice cream parlor with the sign made of faux cones of chocolate, vanilla, and strawberry with black eyes and noses on their scoops and hats atop them. He pulled into a space right in front of it and hurried inside. No Gwenie. He fast-stepped outside. The fountain spewed pink, blue, and yellow sprays into a pond surrounded by yellow daisies as though the world hadn't stopped spinning.

Fred's place, Dad's grocery, sat next door. Posters advertising fresh green beans, corn and squash decorated the big glass windows. Gwenie often shopped here for her mom. The terrible truth hit him in the gut. He hadn't been thinking clearly. Gwenie wouldn't leave the hospital and go anywhere in town. Someone had taken her. But who? Could it have been the bully from the restaurant?

He hurried back to the car, got in, and gripped the steering wheel so tight his fingers ached as he backed out. A short trip down Main Street took him to the steep highway, where he zoomed to the dirt road, turned, and then slowed down. Keep it steady driving over the ruts and rocks. Another wreck would delay his search.

Thick leaves on the tall, old trees blocked some of the sunlight until he approached the spot where he'd crashed. The uprooted sycamore tree was gone. Sunshine burst onto that desolate, forsaken underbrush as he pulled in.

His head throbbed as he got out and shut the door, his nerves racing faster than his body could move along the bumpy road. No one could know he was here. If only his mind wasn't so muddled.

The fallen branches from the wreck lay at his feet. They'd hide the banged-up piece of junk he once loved so much. A few squats and a swift arrangement of the limbs and leaves over the vehicle, and he had his camouflage. Would the large burly man ride by and notice someone had filled in the recent gap in the dense forest? Jack would have to take that chance.

The underbrush behind the pines and the hardwoods with heavy leaves hid him as he plodded to the restaurant. Soon the shades of green looked the same in every direction, and he lost his bearings. If he walked to the left, he should see the road. He took a step and froze. Four-toed tracks. Where was it? Something rustled beside him. A deer loped out of the lush foliage across a large log.

A low guttural growl. Louder. In front of him. He stood on his tip-toes, took off his black jacket and spread it between his arms high above his head. The reddish-brown catamount hissed and opened its huge mouth lined with razor sharp teeth. A roar erupted, and horror raced through every fiber of Jack's being. He made eye contact with the animal without moving his head. Every muscle in his body tugged at him to collapse.

The catamount snarled as his yellow-brown eyes seemed to stare right through him. He trembled as the huge feline slung its head and bounded toward him. He stopped breathing.

The animal's bad breath hit him in the face. Could it smell fear? The throaty roar commenced again. The beast of prey darted to the left of Jack and crouched.

Jack breathed in then slowly turned his head. The deer leapt through the forest. The predator sprang forward, defined muscles bulging in its sleek body as it vaulted into the chase. Limbs snapping and underbrush rustling echoed in the distance. Jack plopped down on the log, sucked in a few deep breaths, and revved up his nerve with thoughts of Gwenie's sweet smile.

He stood and stepped cautiously to the left, staying behind the shield of trees close to the road until he saw the restaurant at the bottom of the hill. Gwenie was right. No marque or signage. Derick's Down-Home Dining sat void of visible cars and people. Still, Jack kept out of sight as he trod to the edge of the gravel parking lot.

Cool air wafted from the stream behind the building, the smell of damp moss and grass tickling his nostrils as he ventured to the back of the structure. He squatted and waddled like a duck to the panoramic window, leaned over, and peeked in. No one inside. Right again, Gwenie. This was not a public establishment. Was she locked in the building somewhere?

A familiar rattle sounded in the distance. Jack peered around the corner at the black truck bumping down the road. He glanced at the thick forest then the clearing between him and the trees. Not enough time to cross.

The vehicle rumbled closer.

He thrust his foot onto the bottom log where the lumber met at the corner of the house then scaled the building as easily as a slider slipping up a zipper. The truck stopped as he hoisted himself onto the gray slate covering. Thankful for his climbing experience, he lay as flat as he could while peering down.

The vehicle's door swung open, and the big guy with the black eyes stepped out as his cell phone rang. He reached in his shirt pocket with his huge hand and grabbed it. "Yeah."

Jack scooted closer to the ridge.

"Naw, I didn't bring her to the cabin. That stupid kid hit a tree leaving here. His car's all banged up. The girl was knocked out, and the kid looked like he was just coming to when I asked if I could help. Huh?" Silence. "They'd had to call a wrecker and who knows who else if I hadn't gotten the thing back on the road. As it was—that's what I'm tryin' to tell you. As it was—they had to go to the hospital, and I know they filed a police report. I wouldn't be surprised to see the cops snooping around this place soon. So no—she's at the other house on. Yeah, on top of the mountain. All right. I'm goin' to get the cabin ready for the meeting tomorrow. I'm going back, but she *don't* need a guard. She can't get out of the shack, and if she did, how's she going to get off the mountain?"

The big guy returned his cell phone to his pocket, unlocked the door to the cabin, ducked, and went indoors.

Jack's insides churned like a washing machine as he stepped backward one log at a time. What mountain? A chunk of the material between the cabin's joints fell with a thud. A twig snapped when the soles of Jack's tennis shoes hit the ground.

The sliding glass door next to the panoramic window opened. "Who's out there?"

Jack's pulse quickened as he hurried to the side of the building and squatted down.

Footfalls pounded the deck.

Terror filled Jack's mind. What now? There was no room for error. He had to stay free to rescue Gwenie and save the farm.

Thumps fell closer to the edge of the deck.

He slid underneath it and peered up through a crack between two planks. He wiped sweat off his forehead as the giant-of-a-man poked his head around the corner where Jack had been.

Burly Man stomped on the boards over Jack's hiding spot. "I know someone's out here." The man scanned the backyard then meandered across the deck while staring down. His footfalls grew louder, his focus closer.

Jack stopped breathing.

A possum ran from the woods across the gravel onto the deck.

Burly Man picked it up and clamped its jaws shut. The rodent stared at Burly Man with beady eyes while Jack exhaled slowly.

"Ah, you ain't hurtin' nothin.' I'll let you go, but don't come around here again. I thought you wuz squirt, or worse, a cop."

The big guy threw the possum so far into the woods Jack didn't see it land. He lay limp as Burly Man walked in the house and shut the door. His spirit wanted to break free, but reason told him to stay put.

The sun sank lower in the sky while loud music rocked the cabin. Jack wiggled his arms and legs to keep blood circulating and his muscles from cramping. He shook his hands up and down to shoo away bugs. The sky grew dim, and he wondered what Gwenie was doing. How was Dad? Twilight gave way to night and the stars lit the Heavens.

Finally the lights shining through the panoramic window from inside shut off and the music stopped. Jack wiggled his feet and legs out from under the deck as spotlights lit up the parking lot as bright as day. He squatted down behind the back wall at the corner of the cabin. An engine roared then rattled. Was it safe to leave?

Chapter Ten - The Undercover Operation

Pounding footsteps echoed in Gwenie's brain. Was she having a nightmare? She forced her heavy eyelids open and stared into the dark room. The only light shone through tiny cracks in between gray plank walls. Where were the white walls? The shadow? Oh no. She remembered. She was in a ram-shackled room with Burly Man. She rubbed her head.

"Hullo Sweet Cakes. I didn't forget about you." His voice boomed into the black silence.

Gwenie's heart raced like a motor turned on high. If she'd ever been this frightened, she couldn't recall a time.

Burly Man flipped a switch on the wall. He stepped into dim light spreading over part of the room and plodded to her.

"Look at you. All that beautiful long, auburn hair a mess. Those green eyes wide as plates on pale skin. I ain't gonna' hurt you. I didn't even tie you up. No need up here. Nothing but a helicopter comes to the top of this mountain since the road washed out. Soon as Jack's old man sells the farm, you can leave. Now if he *don't*... we won't talk about that just yet."

"Was I in a helicopter?"

"Yep. Between the bump on your head and the chloroform, no wonder you don't remember nothin'."

"I remember plenty. I'll be leaving soon."

The big man knitted his dark, bushy eyebrows. "Now, don't get smart again."

If he thought that was smart, he ought to hear what she was thinking. He was the most obnoxious excuse for a human being she'd ever seen with his yellow teeth and bad breath, not to mention he was as clumsy as a dinosaur on tranquilizers. "Sorry. It won't happen again."

"I thought we wuz going to be friends."

Was he crazy? "Sure. I make friends with all my kidnappers."

Burly Man raised his hairy eyebrows. "What'd I just say?"

"Okay, if we're friends, could I have some water, please?"

"Yes, ma'am, where'd my manners go? You hungry?"

Gwenie's stomach turned. "No thank you, just the water."

The beast ambled out of the room, returned, and handed a glass to Gwenie. Then he sat down in a flowered, tattered upholstered chair the size of a love seat, his hips filling the entire area. He held up a glass the size of a tea pitcher. "Bottoms up."

Gwenie's hand shook as she toasted the brute before she took a sip. The water soothed her dry mouth, but did nothing for her exploding headache, not to mention the fear going off inside her like firecrackers on July fourth.

An owl moaned " whooo" outside while Burly Man stared at her, gulping his drink, his slurping the only sound in the deadly quiet room. Gwenie tried to scoot out of the yellow circular glow cast by the light. She wished she could make herself small like a moth and fly away.

"I'm sure enjoying looking at you. It ain't every night I have a beautiful damsel up here." His low, guttural voice resounded in the room.

Gwendolyn's stomach roiled. "Where's up here?"

"You think I'm dumb. I ain't saying. You'll send squirt a text. That reminds me—" He held out a hand the size of a saucer, dark hair on his knuckles. "Give me the cell phone."

"It was in my purse, but I lost it."

Burly Man stood, his head nearly touching the ceiling. He marched across the room and returned with Gwenie's small black pocketbook. He threw everything on the floor one item at a time. "Do you want me to come over there and find it?"

Gwenie's heart sank as she shook her head. "Out with it."

Burly Man blinked his eyes, and Gwenie yanked the cell phone from her bra. She held out her hand. "Here."

Burly Man's eyes widened. "What else do you have hidden?" He took two steps and stood in front of her. "This calls for a body search." His breathing grew heavy then he snorted, his thick upper lip curling on the right then heavy breathing, snorting, more heavy breathing.

***

Jack eventually slid out from under the deck, his heart beating in his throat as he stood. The bright spotlight glowed on the gravel parking lot and lit a row of trees in the forest. It was the middle of the night. Only this morning he'd picked up Gwenie in his new red car, and now she'd been kidnapped. Burly Man was the key. Where had he gone? To a house on a mountain? That could be anywhere. Jack peered around the corner.

Shining a small pocket flashlight he ran as fast as he could from the cabin to the road then to the car. He took a sigh of relief. The hardwoods and pines he'd used to camouflage the banged-up vehicle looked like part of the forest. Apparently Burly Man had thought so too, or he would have searched for Jack.

He lifted the branches and threw them aside as fast as his hands would move. He opened the creaky door, got in, and backed onto the bumpy dirt road. His headlights danced on the trees as he snaked his way up the earthen path. An eerie silence hung in the air.

He had to sleep, even if only for an hour or two. With every muscle in his body he yearned to find Gwenie right now, but his eyelids drooped as though they had weights tied to them and his head ached. What good would it do to start his search exhausted and not be able to finish it? It was so dark, and which way would he go? He knew of no house on a mountain.

No lights shone from the shops and no water squirted from the fountain as he pulled onto the highway leading into town. Neon lights blinked on the marque in front of Philips Clothing and Fairy Wings Mercantile.

Aside from Jack's grandmother and grandfather no one in his family had earned their wings. Soon his dad and mom would have the honor. When a Fairwilde resident reached sixty, if he or she had enough good deeds on his or her community help record, bingo. That person received wings to display on the house, car, or business. Jack's heart sank. Dad must be in so much pain.

It seemed hours, but was probably only twenty minutes, before he turned onto the road leading to Greenthumb Acres. The moon shone over miles of green beans. To stay awake he tried to remember which vegetable field came next. The corn, next the squash, the peas.

He wheeled into the circular drive in front of the big white plantation home and cut the engine.

The wide gray steps seemed a hurdle too difficult to cross. He put one determined foot in front of the other and plodded up them. He trod across the matching porch to the white beveled door, slipped in his key, and collapsed on the parquet floor in the foyer.

***

A loud noise buzzed through Jack's brain like a chainsaw. Where was he? What day was it? The white foyer wall and green silk tree in the corner came into focus as he sat up. The racket came from his cell phone. He rubbed his eyes and reached in his pocket. Tuesday, June 2nd. Oh no, he'd slept six hours. Nearly nineteen had gone by since someone attacked Dad and kidnapped Gwenie. He had to find her.

"Hello."

"Hi, son."

Panic raced through him like electricity. It was Mom. "Is everything all right?"

"It's great. Dad's going home. We have to wait here for the doctor to sign us out. It'll be about three hours. Will you meet us at the house?"

So much hope and excitement rang in Mom's voice. He couldn't tell her he had something else to do. He could make a trip to the outskirts of town then get back here in less than three hours. "Did you need me to pick you up at the hospital?"

"No, an orderly will bring Daddy out to the car, and I can drive us home.

"All right, I'll see you at Greenthumb Acres in three hours."

"Perfect."

They hung up, the cheer from Mom's voice lingering over Jack, lifting his spirits. It took a load off his mind to know Dad was well enough to come home, but fear for Gwenie ran through every nerve in his body.

He rushed up the oak staircase to his room and yanked off his clothes, tossing them on the brown carpet. A few steps took him to the bathroom where he washed his face and brushed his teeth. The beige and brown fluffy pillows on his bed beckoned to him as he forced his feet into the bedroom and to his chest.

The morning sun pouring in the window glinted off his gold and silver rock climbing trophies as he pulled out a pair of black jeans. They reminded him at least he had the expertise to get up a mountain. If he only knew which one to climb.

He rummaged for the black tee shirt imprinted with a skull and the scarring liquid he'd used in a community play this past winter. Fifteen minutes in front of the mirror to add makeup, and he walked away sporting a big scar running down the side of his face.

He had plenty of time to get to Rochester and return home before Mom and Dad arrived. If only he could make his act seem real. He rushed outside, stopped short of the banged-up car then hopped into one of the white and green Greenthumb Acres vans.

A short ride took him to the back road leading to the land of the dark. The clumsy vehicle bumped along the dirt path lined with oak and maple trees and unkempt underbrush. He drove as fast as he could. Dust flew as he neared the black gate that kept un-wanted, un-loved, un-savory people at bay. A lump of fear rose in his throat as he parked underneath two oak trees with huge roots. Only the love burning in his heart for Gwenie fueled his courage.

A walk through prickly bushes that snagged his pants took him to the side of the fence, where he squatted down and pulled his iPhone out of his jeans pocket. Using the binocular app, he zeroed in on the entrance, searching for the guard, his nerves as jagged as the barbed wire in front of him. Couldn't miss him—two hundred or more pounds, bulging in khakis and a matching shirt. He walked around a wooden perch above the yard with a gun at his waist. Sneaking around would be easier at night, but Jack didn't have time to wait. At least he probably peered at a relaxed sentry. He'd hardly expect anyone to break into Rochester at all, much less during the day.

Jack touched a metal prong to the bottom rung of the gate and jumped. An electrical shock ripped through his exhausted body. He wasn't going over the top. What about hidden lasers that set off alarms? His insides churned as he dug underneath the barrier with the prong and his hands while staring at the officer pacing back and forth.

The lookout stopped and got out his binoculars, rotating his body as though he scanned the area.

Jack lay face down in the dirt, fear rushing through his veins like the Awasai in a storm. He turned his head enough to peep until the sentry pivoted toward the other side of the field. He mashed his body close to the ground, sucked in air, and held his breath as he reached his arms underneath the fence to the other side. Grabbing hold of a volcanic rock the same color as his clothes he pulled through with his heart thumping like a rabbit jumping. The rotund watchman glanced his way.

He stayed as still as the stone, peering out of the corner of his eye until the sentinel turned. He exhaled, terror knotting his stomach while visions of Gwenie pushed him onward. He ran and hid behind a large holly bush, smoothing his pants and pushing back his hair. He took a deep breath and checked out the yard.

Fifty feet away a group of men huddled together. He dashed to a maple tree halfway between them and him, leaned against the back of it, and spotted a dumpster only ten feet from the inmates. He charged to it as fast as his black boots would take him, his pulse quickening. Show time.

He crept to the front of the garbage repository, puffed out his chest, and put a swagger in his walk as he headed toward the gangsters. A couple of men meandered into a large one-story building, leaving only three. Jack's eye twitched as he bounded into their conversation, but he focused on overcoming his fear by acting as though he belonged here. Nodding his head when they spoke, he listened to the slang they used.

"Hey kiddo, what's your name? I'm Milton," the red-head said.

"Where'd you come from?" The hoodlum with long, stringy blond hair stared at him as though he wanted a reason to take all his anger out on Jack.

Jack concentrated on hiding the trembling rocking his insides. "One question at a time, I'm Lloyd the Snake. I come from Fairwilde. I got caught pushin' a little white powder."

Milton and the blond-haired guy laughed.

Milton pointed to a man with a bushy black beard. "That's Ralph."

Ralph tapped Jack on the arm. "You bring any with you?"

Jack and the others laughed, and Jack breathed easier.

"That's a good one," Jack said. "I might have a connection when I get outta' here though. I got some stuff from this huge guy in Fairwilde. I'd never seen him before. If I knew where to find him I could buy more." Jack's voice radiated the confidence he'd intended despite his unhinged nerves.

Milton stuck out his lower lip as he squinted. "Why can't you see him where you met him?"

"Cause, I was in the woods with my girl." Jack snickered. "We wuz havin' a little fun, and here he comes out of nowhere wantin' to know if I'd like a shot of something."

Ralph glanced at Milton. "That musta' been the big kid workin' with Tim and Fancy Frogs at that old restaurant."

Jack nodded. "I took the girl home then went back to the woods. I banged on the door at the cabin, but no one was there. Then I left and pulled onto the highway. This cop busted me for speeding."

"I hate that." Wrinkles creased Milton's brow. "We might be able to help you find this guy if you can prove you're one of us. You just going to do your time, get out, and blab to the cops, or are you with us for life?"

"I'm with you, man. I'm with you."

Milton, Ralph, and the blond-haired guy stared at Jack. "Prove it. If you talked to the big guy you know our motto."

Panic wiped Jack's mind as blank as a clean blackboard.

"He ain't one of us." The blond-haired guy threw up his arms.

Jack noticed a B cut into his bicep. "Anybody got a knife."

"No, dumb-bell. The guard pats us down every day." Milton tilted his head. "You don't have ta' do it. Just tell us what it stands for."

The blond-haired man got right in Jack's face. "And get it right the first time, or you might find yourself in a heap for lying to us. They can't take away our hands." He held out a large, rough pair. They looked as though they'd been broken in several places.

Jack's mind froze like a block of ice.

"We're waitin." Ralph knitted his dark, bushy eyebrows.

Oh, dear Lord, help me. The B had to be for bad something, but what? When Gwenie was knocked out in the car, and the big man helped them, he'd said something weird. "Bad—Bad to the Gut."

The blond's eyes snapped wide.

Ralph grinned big. "All right. When you get out of here, get in touch with Tim. You can find him at the restaurant. He'll take you to their hide-out on Mount Morgan in his helicopter."

Relief coursed through every bone in Jack's body. He knew exactly which peak it was.

"Tell him you want more stuff for Milton, Ralph and Yerof." Ralph pointed to the blond-haired guy. "He's Yerof."

Jack was as limp as a cooked noodle. "Hi."

Yerof shrugged his shoulders. "Hullo."

Wrinkles creased Ralph's brow as though he resented the interruption even though he'd introduced him to Yerof. "After you get it, bring it to the guard that's here at three o'clock in the morning. He's got blond spiked hair. If he wasn't in his uniform you'd think he was one of us." Ralph gestured with his palm out. "Just give him our secret message. If the guard *don't* know how to answer, he ain't the right one. You'll have ta' come back."

Yerof nodded. "Right. Tell him you know it's the middle of the night, but you're not going to be able to make the seven o'clock delivery, so you're bringing it now. He'll tell you it's all right he'll take care of it. Got it?"

Jack tried to keep his eyes from widening. They were criminals. What'd he expect? "Yes."

Ralph relaxed his stiff stance. "When you gettin' out. When can you bring it?" A hint of friendliness lined his voice.

"It's a first offense. Could be as early as tomorrow."

Ralph, Milton, and Yerof started laughing, giving each other light taps on their biceps and high-fiving each other.

Ralph stopped clowning around. "So, how long after you leave here?"

Jack shrugged. "Say it's tomorrow, I'll look for Tim the day after, and have him take me to the mountain."

Ralph slapped him on the back. "All right, let's go inside."

"I'm going to stay out a little longer. Commune with nature."

"Man, you're weird, but that's okay." Ralph put his hand on top of Jack's then slid it off slow and easy. "Bad to the Gut."

Milton and Yerof followed suit, Jack repeating "Bad to the Gut" to each of them. They walked off and Jack lay flat on the ground as still as a mouse.

He got his iPhone out of his jeans' pocket and peered at the guard. Sweet. His back was toward him. He ran to the dumpster. Then the big man on the perch turned in Jack's direction. Jack panted, his heartbeat accelerating, sweat popping out on his forehead. His hands went numb. What was happening to him?

He had to take control for Gwenie. An image of her auburn hair blowing in the wind flashed in his mind and his breathing leveled out. He tried to wiggle his fingers. Yes. He pressed his body against the earth and inched a little at a time to the maple tree then to the holly bush and underneath the fence. He thanked God for helping him and for the athletic ability that let him slip past the electric barrier. Then he filled in the hole he'd dug and put grass, weeds, and twigs on top of it.

He fast-stepped to the van, got in, and chugged down the road to go home to see Mom and Dad. He'd been gone two hours and fifteen minutes. He had time to spare. Bouncing over ruts and rocks, he nearly jumped out of his skin for wanting to get to the shack.

Chapter Eleven - The Rescue Plan

Jack returned the company van to the back of the house. Pulling it in beside another one just like it, he parked. He slammed the door and charged across the lush green yard into the kitchen, his pulse pounding from head to toe. He couldn't wait to climb that mountain.

Bertille stared at him with wide eyes. "Oh, Mister Jack, you're home?" Her voice shook.

"Yes."

Bertille put her hand around her waist and rocked back and forth in the wide stripe the sun made shining in the window.

"What's wrong?"

She ventured to the front of the house, Jack on her heels. Clearing the hall and the foyer, she flung open the door. "Look, someone ruined all the vegetables."

Shock hit Jack like a board to his stomach. "What are you talking about Bertille? I came by the crops in the middle of the night, and they were fine.

"They ain't now. Oh Heaven help us. Your daddy and mama are going to be so upset."

Jack put his arm around Bertille.

She stared at him with longhorn steer tears leaking from her eyes.

Jack gazed out the window at the chopped up green beans, pieces of leaves and stalks from the vines all mixed up with chunks of squash like an enormous salad. How had he slept through such a massacre? He'd never been as tired in his life, but surely he would have heard something. Later this morning he'd gone out the backdoor straight to the van and left driving away from the fields.

"You gonna' phone the cops? Your daddy can't be bothered with this, him in the hospital and all."

"You're exactly right, as usual." Jack reached in his pocket and pulled out the card Captain Jones had given him. "I'll call, but Dad's on his way home."

"No!" Bertille grasped her waist and started rocking again. "He can't see this. What are we going to tell your parents?"

"From the looks of things out there, we won't have to tell them anything. They're going to see it, but try not to worry. Dad's a strong man."

Jack's stomach churned like the hay baler as he dialed the numbers. Three rings. He told Captain Jones what had happened and hung up. "The captain's on his way."

Bertille nodded. " Good. That's a start. I'm going to try and get some cleanin' done." She left the room, and Jack plopped down in a straight-back chair that matched the large round oak table in the kitchen and wrung his hands.

He had to get out of here and find Gwenie, but Mom and Dad needed his help. His brain turned to scrambled eggs as he leaned back in the chair and put his hands over his head.

"Mister Jack, come quick. Mr. Flourez needs you."

Jack sprang out of his chair and rushed to the foyer.

Fernando peered at him with dark anxious eyes as he twirled his brown felt hat around and around in front of his slim body. "It's awful, Mister Jack. Just awful."

Jack's heart fell to his toes. "What now? I already know about the vegetables."

"It's the flowers in the hot houses, the beautiful orchids, the roses—" Fernando wiped sweat off his brow. Some of them are broken and torn. I don't know how many I can save."

"What about the fruit?"

"Yes, so much ruined. What do you want me to do?"

"Are the hot houses intact?"

"Sort of. Someone threw bricks through some of the panels and busted them."

Jack's heart beat against his chest like a drum. Their livelihood, and the entire town's food supply depended on Greenthumb Acres. He had to preserve it for Dad and Fairwilde. "I've already called the police. Don't touch anything until Captain Jones sees the damage. After that I want you and your employees to gather the fruits, vegetables and flowers that can be preserved. Fix anything that can be repaired and still grow, but for now why don't you go in the kitchen and ask Bertille to make a large pot of coffee then have a cup?"

Bertille ran into the foyer, gasping for air. "Mr. Kasey's at the kitchen door. Someone's gone and wrecked the vegetable factory." Tears ran down Bertille's pale cheeks.

A head rush hit Jack as his mom's sedan pulled up in the circular drive in front of the house. "Ask Bob to come in too. Tell him to stay here until Captain Jones finishes his inspection."

"Mister Jack, you're white as a snow. I'm going to get you some water. Go in the den and sit down."

"Bertille, I have to help Dad."

"Right now, you can't help nobody." Bertille took hold of Jack's arm and led him to the green leather sofa in the den. "Stay put 'till I get back. Fernando can help your papa. I'm going to get you a drink."

Bertille was right. The built-in walnut bookcases on either side of the big-screen television blurred as the room spun.

"Mister Jack. Mister Jack. Can you take hold of this?" Betille's voice wafted from a distance.

Black.

***

Jack was so cold. A strong ammonia odor nearly gagged him. He jumped and opened his eyes. Bertille swiped a rag filled with crushed ice across his forehead and held smelling salts under his nose.

He pushed her small hand away. "Bertille, I'm fine. Where are Dad and Mom?"

Dad sat beside him, smiling as he patted Jack's knee with his right hand. "It's all right, son. Everything's going to be fine."

Screams resounded in Jack's head, but he tried to speak calmly. "No Dad, the farm's ruined, you're beaten up, and Gwenie's missing." Ooops. He hadn't meant to bother Mom and Dad with his and Gwenie's problem. He had intended to take care of things here then get Gwenie.

Dad sat up as though someone stuck him with a pin. "Ouch." He grimaced as he touched his ribs. "What are you talking about, son?"

He might as well tell Dad. "I heard a man tell George…you know who owns the body shop?"

"Yes." Jack's dad peered at him with questioning blue eyes.

"This guy raved to George about Derick's Down Home Dining. I took Gwenie there to eat. Of all things, a man demanded I tell you to sell the farm. I know it sounds crazy, but I think he took Gwenie from the hospital."

Dad cocked an eyebrow. "I have to sell to get back Gwenie?"

"Right. No. That's what they want, but I have a plan."

"Okay, son, start from the beginning."

"Derick's Down Home Dining is in a cabin set up like a restaurant, but I'm convinced it's not for the public. Yesterday, I went back and snooped around. While I was there, the man who insisted you sell returned. He told someone on his cell phone he'd taken "her" to the house on the mountain. I bet "her" is Gwenie."

Jack's voice cracked as his heart broke into a million pieces, but he tried to keep his composure as he explained. "I'm going to get her." He swallowed a knot in his throat. "But I have to find out exactly where the place is." He wasn't about to tell his mom and dad he'd spent part of the day in Rochester and upset them even more. "I think it might be on Mount Morgan." Jack wiped his forehead. "I have to do something about the farm. I've called Captain Jones."

Dad picked up a brown mug from the coffee table with his right hand. "That was the best thing you could've done for us. I drove to the factory and the hot houses as soon as we got here while you and Bertille were still in the kitchen talking to Fernando. We pulled over to the house, and Captain Jones parked in the drive right behind us. I asked him to check out both places." Dad took a sip of his drink. "Don't worry. I have insurance. I'll get Greenthumb Acres up and running again before we know it. It's Gwenie we need to worry about."

Mom who sat in the green and brown easy chair on the other side of Dad nodded. "Yes, we've had worse problems than this. One year when you were a toddler drought dried up the river. We thought we'd lose everything, but God sent rain and we made it through. It wasn't a big crop, but we did all right. The Lord will take care of our farm. Have you told Captain Jones about Gwenie?"

"I told him she was missing, but I haven't said anything about the restaurant."

Mom tapped her forefinger to her lips. "I haven't thought of it in a long time, but there used to be an old house on the top of Mount Morgan."

Dad scratched his left arm underneath the edge of his cast. "No one's been up there in years. That winding path they called a road is closed."

Adrenaline pumped through Jack's veins. "I could scale it. It wouldn't take me long."

Bertille strolled in with a tray of sandwiches.

A wave of nausea swept over Jack as she stuck it in front of him.

"Mister Jack. You have to eat something."

Jack gave her the most pitiful expression he could manage and rubbed his stomach. "I can't."

She pushed the tray closer to him. "Eat."

"You can't climb on an empty stomach." Dad touched Jack's arm, and Jack took the sandwich.

"That has to be the place. I know Fairwilde Kingdom well, and that's the only shack on a mountain anywhere around here. It's been abandoned ever since old Mister Gubb died." Dad sat back.

Mom's blue eyes grew wide as saucers. "No. He's not going. It's too dangerous. Why just getting up there could…" Mom choked up. "How did the hoodlums get up there in the first place?"

Dad took a bite of his sandwich. "Helicopter or small airplane. There's an old runway Mister Gubb used to call an air strip on top of the mountain. It's short, but it's flat."

"Don't anybody move. I'll be right back." Bertille left and returned with Fernando.

He twirled his hat.

Bertille cut her brown eyes toward him. "Tell them."

"Since green beans are our biggest crop, I mess around with seeds in the green house, just for fun."

Dad leaned forward. "And."

Fernando tilted his head and smiled. "I know you ain't gonna believe this, but about a week ago I got some seeds from a man in town. I sowed one at the base of Mount Morgan in the fertile bottomland to see if it'd grow fast like the man said." Fernando's dark eyes widened. "I was afraid to tell you because I didn't know how to stop it. The other day I took a chainsaw to it."

Bertille hopped from one foot to the other. "Don't you see, Mister Jack could climb up and get Miss Gwenie."

"Bertille." Disbelief rang in Mom's loud voice.

Bertille lowered her head and ran from the room as though she couldn't stand that she'd displeased Mom.

"Now look what you've done." Dad cut an accusing eye at Mom.

"Jack's not going to rescue anyone. He's only a boy." Mom's usually soft tone sounded razor sharp.

Fernando peered at Mom with compassionate eyes. "'Scuse me, but he could get there lots quicker than the police. They're still outside taking molds of tire tracks, dusting for fingerprints. Who knows what they're doing? It takes them forever to gather evidence before they start to work. Miss Gwenie might need Jack now. He could save her life, and the plant's safe. I promise. Who would suspect anyone entering a shack on a mountain by climbing up a beanstalk?"

Bertille ran in the room screaming and holding out a piece of paper to Dad. "Look. This was lying on the back porch. We musta' missed it in all the hullabaloo. It says the farm and Gwenie are just wake-up calls. If you don't sell the land, they're going to kill all of you starting with Gwenie."

Anger boiled inside Jack like an over-heated pot of water, bubbling through his veins. "Just let them try."

Tears ran down Mom's cheeks.

Jack got up and hugged her. "It'll be fine, and no one's going to kill any of us."

Steel-strong strength shown in Dad's eyes. "Fernando, check out that stem and let Jack know when it's ready for climbing."

Chapter Twelve - Getting to Know Noble

Gwenie dared not faint. Yet the tattered sofa was fading, her mind drifting, a musty smell smothering her. Where was she? She blinked her eyes. Her captor hovered over her, his lip snarling, shades of gray filling the window behind him as this dark night in the shack dissipated. What was happening? If only she could remember.

He'd thrown everything out of her purse looking for her cell phone. What had he said? "What do you mean you want to be friends?"

He stood back. "You're going to be my buddy?"

" Sure…" He wanted her to call him—what was it? "Yes Noble, but you'll have to act like a gentleman." "Friends" could mean different things to people. Gwenie wanted him to know that to her, it meant he respected her.

He plopped down in the huge chair and shook his head, his dark bushy hair bouncing back

and forth across his face. "I've always wanted
pals," he whispered.

A twinge of hope hit Gwenie, and her taut
muscles relaxed/ She scooted to the edge of the gray
sofa, and stuck out her hand, holding it as steady as
she could. "You have one now."

Noble grinned, leaned forward, and shook it.

She sat back. "What about the people at
Derick's Down-Home Dining? Aren't they your
friends?"

Noble frowned. "No. I work for them. They
pay me to pick up heavy boxes, mop the floors, or
whatever else they tell me to do."

"Did they tell you to bring me here?"

Noble hung his head and the rising sun
beamed onto it from the high window. At last the
worst night of Gwenie's life was over.

"Yes. I didn't think you'd want to come, and
I didn't want to hurt you." Noble leaned over her.

Her nerves shook as though they were in a
blender.

"Honest. I haven't hurt you, have I? You
want something to eat? They told me I could give
you a sandwich."

Nausea climbed in Gwenie's throat, but
eating a sandwich for breakfast was much better
than getting snarled at, or worse, attacked. "Yes,
please. Do you want me to help fix it?"

"No. They told me not to let you off the sofa
except to go to the bathroom."

"I went once while you were asleep."
Gwenie bit her tongue. She hadn't meant to sound
defiant. Was he angry?

"That's okay. We can't escape from the
mountain. They just want you where they can get
you out in a hurry when they come."

"Who are they?"

"Some guys I went to school with over in
Rochester Kingdom."

Gwenie gasped. It was the most horrible
place in all of Fairwilde. The rogues, criminals, and
scientific experiments gone bad lived there. "How
did you end up in Rochester?"

"They only looked at my outside. No one
paid any attention to my heart. Look at me. I'm a
monster." Noble's dark evil eyes turned sad and
misty. "Sometimes I have flashbacks and remember
when my heart was free."

"When was that?"

Noble's lips turned up on the corners.
"When my brother, Joe, took care of me. He'd gone
to live with my Aunt Mary, and I went to visit him.
Joe and I played with building blocks Aunt Mary
bought for us. We went to Vacation Bible School.
That's where I learned about God and not to hurt
people. At first the kids were afraid of me, but I
picked them up and swung them around and they
loved it. Aunt Mary and Joe loved me."

"Why did you leave?"

Noble's lips turned down. "She couldn't
afford to keep two boys all the time. I had to come

home and go to school. I was so much bigger than everyone else. The kids didn't want to be around me. I wouldn't have harmed them, but they ran away before I could tell them. Fancy Frogs and Tim Berkowitz, the waiter at the cabin, were in my class. They played with me.

Tim's part of the gang too, but he stutters something awful. They don't let him talk to people. Anyway, we started hanging out in third grade and got into trouble in high school. They robbed a gas station when the attendant went to the men's room. I drove the get-away car, so they sent us all to Rochester. I've been there ever since."

"What about your parents? Didn't they get you out of there?"

"No. They had so many kids they didn't need a monster like me."

How sad that he had to leave his aunt and brother who loved him. Gwenie sat up like she'd gotten stuck with a pin. "Someone loves you even more than Aunt Mary and Joe."

Noble cocked his head and gave her a puppy dog look. "Who?"

"The Lord. Turn this over to Him." Gwenie was going to say God could do anything, but Noble interrupted her.

"The Lord don't want nothin' to do with the likes of me now that I've lived in Rochester."

A yearning to let Noble know God loved him filled Gwenie. "Don't say that. It's not true. We're all God's children. He cares about each of us.

All you have to do is accept His love, study His
Word, and turn your life around."

Noble stared at her with questioning eyes.
"How do I do that?"

"Read the Bible and go to church."

"We ain't got churches in Rochester."

"Don't stay there. Come to Fairwilde
Community Church. If you'll change your ways, the
people there will be friends."

"I'd like that." Noble got a faraway look in
his eyes.

Noble's phone rang. "Hullo. Oh hi, Boss.
Yep. She's right here on the sofa waitin' on me to
get her a sandwich. What? No, of course, there's no
one here, but us. Who do you think could come to
the top of this mountain without a helicopter? I got
ya'. If I see a helicopter, I get out the high-powered
rifle and shoot it down. Bang. Bang."

Gwenie turned limp, slumping on the sofa,
trying to stay conscious.

Noble clicked off the phone and tossed it on
the coffee table. "All right. I'll get your food."

She had to stay alert and talk to Noble.
"Wait. You can't shoot down a helicopter. What if
it crashed and killed someone? You'd be a
murderer. Right now, you're just a kidnapper, and I
don't have to press charges."

Noble's mouth gaped. "You'd do that for
me?"

"Sure. If you let me go and don't hurt anyone else. What have you done besides kidnap me?"

"You were my first job, well other than driving the car for the robbery. They said I was incompetent because we got caught. Since then they just let me do heavy work. I built the restaurant with my bare hands."

Visions of the fine workmanship on the paneling inside the dining room flashed in Gwenie's head. "Tell me about it."

Noble shook his head. "It's mostly for the hoods in Rochester. It's not really for outsiders, but they told me to go to town and figure out a way to get Jack in there. First thing I tried, talking about it in front of him, worked."

Jack had so much to learn. "So, it does operate as an eatery."

Noble's eyes widened. "Oh yeah. We got plenty of food. The gangs come pretty regular."

"What about other people?"

"So far, just you and Jack."

"What's in the heavy boxes?"

"I dunno." Noble rubbed his chin."I better get your sandwich. I'm glad we're going to be friends." Noble touched Gwenie's hair as he walked past her, and her skin crawled. She'd thought he'd act like a gentleman since they were buddies. "You're so beautiful." He left the room. She told herself he'd only meant a pat on the head.

Bangs and clangs echoed from the kitchen behind Gwenie. "Are you sure you don't want some help?"

"No ma'am. Remember, you can't get off the sofa except to go to the bathroom. Try to stay comfortable. I'm comin.'"

A few more thumps and thuds then Noble strolled in carrying a blue platter. Two pimento cheese sandwiches jammed against each other lay on it, lettuce sticking out the sides. He handed it to her. "I made you one just like mine. I figured you'd be hungry. We ain't had nothin' to eat since we got here."

Gwenie took the serving tray and set it on the laminated coffee table, the rickety piece of furniture shifting. She'd be lucky if she got down three bites.

"You're lookin' at it weird." Noble snapped his fingers. "I know. I didn't bring you nuthin' to drink. Don't you worry. I got plenty of pop, tea, lemonade. Which do you want?"

"Tea, please."

"Comin' right up."

Noble left, returned, and handed her a pitcher of tea. "Like mine."

She might be able to get down the tea. She was thirsty. "What about the bathroom? I need to go again."

"Yeah. You can go, but I have to walk you to the door and stand outside. If you stay in there too long I have ta' come in and get you."

Anger shot up Gwenie's spine like a flame. "I don't think that'll be necessary." She spoke in as stern a tone as she could manage, got up, stretched, and meandered to the door. Her head ached. She glared at Noble. "Do not come in here."

She entered the dingy restroom with its yellowed fixtures and got out as fast as she could. Who'd want to stay in there any longer than he or she had to?

Noble smiled when she sat down on the sofa. "Eat."

Gwenie picked up part of a pimento cheese sandwich and nibbled it.

Noble snorted then grasped half of his creation with his large hand and poked most of one sandwich in his mouth. "Umm. Umm." He chewed then slurped some tea. "This is good. Don't you like it?"

"Yes, it's delicious, thank you." Gwenie gagged as she cut her eyes toward the window. Where was Jack?

Chapter Thirteen - The Beanstalk

Excitement pounded in Jack's temples as he rose from the sofa. Fernando stood beside the walnut coffee table holding a three-foot-high light green beanstalk four inches in diameter with wide nodes sticking out from it. Jack ran his hand over it. A little scratchy, but not enough to tear a glove or cut the skin. "This is perfect. These nodules make great stepping stones. The climb won't be nearly as difficult as it would with only a rope." Jack pulled back his shoulders. "But I will purchase some equipment for Gwenie." He stared at the living pole. "It's as though I special-ordered a custom-made coil for this climb."

Fernando's dark eyes sparkled. "You did. That's what happens when we get God involved." He took hold of the big vegetable. "This is from a seed I sowed out by the barn. The one on the mountain's even stronger."

Dad's blue eyes widened as he leaned forward. "How big are the beans?"

Fernando tightened his lips. "Hmm. The size of a banana."

"Wow!" Dad sat back. "Are they tender?"

"I haven't cooked any yet. I don't have a big enough pot."

Jack took the plant out of Fernando's hand. "Cut the chit-chat. When do I go to the mountain?"

Mom's blue eyes flashed. "No. Not you. The police. Fernando can get everything Gwenie will need, but it's much too dangerous for you. These men are hardened criminals. It's a known fact that gangsters living in Rochester arm themselves with machine guns. They kill people." Mom's chattering voice trailed off as though she couldn't say more because she feared Jack would be their next victim.

The last thing he needed was an upset Mom to go with his banged-up dad. "Is this what you talk about in your circle meetings?" Jack chuckled a nervous laugh, hoping to lighten the mood.

"Of course not, but everyone knows that's why they keep the bad guys in Rochester. They're too mean and ruthless to mingle with ordinary, every-day people."

Jack gave his mother a hug. "I'm kidding."

"I won't have it. Let the police handle this." Mom directed her gaze at Fernando.

"Yes ma'am, I'll look into it." Fernando turned to Jack. "I'll check the beanstalk later today. I'd say by the wee hours of the night someone could start climbing."

"Yes, you do that—check the stalk. Then the police can start climbing." Mom sat back in her chair.

Shock rushed through Jack's bones. "It will reach the top of Mount Morgan that quick?"

"It's already nine-tenths of the way up the steep grade."

"What makes it grow so big and fast?" Dad—always the farmer, the entrepreneur. Jack's insides were going to blow up if his father didn't stop asking questions.

"I have to be honest. The man in town said these are special seeds from Heaven. They supposedly spring up one time and keep growing as long as we need them. I didn't know what he meant. Now I do."

Dad rubbed his chin with his good hand. "They must be genetically engineered."

Fernando shook his head. "I dunno."

"A gift from God." Mom got up and touched the stem with her small, thin hand. "Thank you, Lord. Please be with the police. Bring them and Gwenie safely back to us."

Dad squeezed Jack's arm. "Amen."

"Amen," Jack repeated. "I'll go with Fernando to check on the progress."

Fernando sped out the door as Jack grabbed his iPhone off the end table and charged out behind him.

They cleared the thick grassy front yard and cut through the fields of chopped-up useless green beans. They leapt over the furrows through broken, tangled vines and into the woods.

Jack jumped over a boulder and charged after Fernando to a handmade suspension bridge. Planks formed a deck supported by ropes and cables. The sight of the flimsy thing stretching across the Awasi had always stopped Jack in his tracks. Today he shot onto it.

He trembled inside as it swung over huge rocks, prickly bushes, and places where snakes lived, but he thanked God it was there to take him to Gwenie. A brown and white deer ten feet away stared at Jack as he approached the other side. He pounded the earth in a run as he dashed off, and the animal fled.

In what seemed like hours, but probably was only twenty minutes, Fernando and Jack bounded from a world of leaves, briars and flowery brambles to grassy flatland at the base of a majestic mountain rising toward the sky. Jack leaned his head back and gazed up the towering peak, but he couldn't see the shack. He pulled the iPhone from his jacket pocket, peered through the binocular app, and gasped. "There it is."

Fernando shoveled rich, black soil around the base of the beanstalk. "Maybe it will grow even quicker if I add dirt and more water. I dunno,' but these are no ordinary seeds. It won't hurt." Fernando swiped his forehead and swung his hand toward the steep alp. "So many rocks on the precipice. The plant will only take hold where there's soil." Fernando grinned. "Your mom is right. It's a gift from Heaven. Rock can't stop it."

Jack scanned the face of the mountain. "I'll need a helmet with a headlamp, a carabiner for attaching to the rope, climbing shoes, and..." Jack touched his forefinger to his lips. "Then there's an assisted braking belay and camming devices. I have plenty of chalk and an extra harness."

"What's a belay?"

"It's a small ring-like piece of metal that creates tension on a rope. Rock climbers use it when they're bringing someone down. If Gwenie starts falling, and she is tied to me for support, it'll allow me to hold her in place or control the weight of the fall, so she can catch her breath."

"You won't even need to use the cord. You'll see. It'll be like walking down steps."

Fernando's confidence in the unique stalk sent a twinge of assurance coursing through Jack's veins, but he was only too aware of how easily things could go wrong on a climb.

Fernando tightened his lips. "What's a camming device?"

"It's a compact tool that slides into cracks in the surface of the mountain and expands to fill the space, helping to anchor the climber."

"What do you mean anchor?"

"Anchors are the points at which the rope attaches to the rock or a tree."

Fernando smiled revealing a mouthful of straight, white teeth. "I don' think you need any of it." Fernando curled his arm and made his biceps pop up. "The stem is strong. You can *jes* climb up and step back down, no problem. But I'll get all the gear you say."

Fernando brushed off his hands. "You are the rock and mountain climbing champion of Fairwilde. This will be easy for you. I'll walk you back here when the plant's completely grown. Your mama's going to be so angry when she finds out you went instead of the police."

Jack touched Fernando's shoulder. "She'll be fine when we get back. In her heart she probably knows I'm not going to let Gwenie stay on top of that mountain. After all, Mom raised me. "Jack peered through the iPhone then lowered it. "I believe that big vegetable just grew an inch. Look."

Fernando bit his bottom lip. "Hmm, at this rate, I'd say you could start later tonight."

A breeze whipped past and billowed out Jack's jacket. "Tell me when it's ready and I'm here." He put the iPhone to his eyes and stared at the shack, his nerves as sharp as razors because he wasn't there now.

Fernando patted him on the back. "C'mon. Your mom and dad will worry. We need to go back and reassure them, especially your mom. Then you should rest. Eat something. It's going to take lots of energy to climb that steep incline and bring Gwenie down."

"You're right." Guilt stuck Jack's skin like pins. He hadn't done anything to help Dad get settled.

Fernando led Jack over the swaying bridge. They stepped into the forest as a brown rabbit hopped across a patch of green grass. Straightening out the mess at Greenthumb Acres still pressed on his mind. Why not start by devising a plan with Fernando? "Have you had a chance to assess the damage to the hot houses?"

"Yes. I've gone through and ordered new panels for all those broken, and I've cleaned up the glass."

"Were any flowers left intact?"

Fernando hung his head as they neared the spoiled crops. "No, but I've already started to take care of the situation." He glanced at his watch. "By now the farm hands are harvesting all of the vegetables they can."

Jack's spirits soared. "You mean all is not lost."

Fernando pointed to their right toward a squash field. The Greenthumb Acres employees swarmed over the debris, picking up usable vegetables and putting them in sacks. "It will take a lot of work, but we'll save every squash, green bean, and ear of corn we can and get it to market, or your dad's grocery. We'll clean the fields and start over."

Gratefulness filled Jack's heart as he and Fernando stepped over a log onto the grass in the Greenthumb's front yard.

Fernando stopped walking and scratched his head. "In the hot houses I've already fixed the broken shoots and dowels using florist tape on all of the plants I could save. We have lots left, including roses and orchids. I've bound the Phalaenopsis Orchids' broken stalks. The nodes I cut from some of the healthiest ones will form stems. Also, I've ordered some quick-growing Mexican sunflowers, yellow flag iris, snapdragons and black-eyed Susans. We've already made our June deliveries, so we've got a month to get together our next orders. God will see us through this. It will be all right."

Fernando's expertise and help made a knot form in Jack's throat as he walked a little lighter up the steps to the house. "You're a blessing. You know that, right?"

Fernando smiled as he opened the beveled glass front door for Jack.

"We're in the kitchen. I'm fixing lunch." Jack's mom's voice sounded like music to his ears. She stood at the white counter by the refrigerator. "I'm getting food together in case you and Fernando want to wait at the base of the mountain for Gwenie when the policemen bring her down."

"That's a great idea." Strange how some people could know something deep in their soul, but tell themselves it wasn't true then convince others likewise. Did they start to believe the untruth? If so, for now that would be best for Mom."

Dad sat at the round oak table, his color drained, his lips turned down.

Jack tapped him on the shoulder. "Have you been resting? Aren't you supposed to be in the bed?"

Dad propped his elbows on the table. "I'm going as soon as we eat. I've been talking with our clients."

Jack sat down next to him. "I could have done that, Dad. I'll call the rest of them tomorrow. Our staff's taking care of the hot houses and fields. Fernando's saved many of the flowers, and the farm hands are salvaging vegetables."

Dad pulled back, sat up straight, and extended his good hand to Fernando. "Thank you. Mr. Kasey has a repairman working on the machines in the factory. With the help of the wonderful people who work for me, God willing, we may put this broken place together soon."

"'Course we will." Fernando shook Dad's hand.

Mom walked to the oven, pulled out a pot roast, and dipped the vegetables onto a platter.

Dad leaned over in his chair and whispered in Jack's ear. "I want to hear about Gwenie the instant you know anything. What does the climb look like?"

Jack couldn't make his dad believe he wasn't going for Gwenie if he tried. Deep inside

Dad probably knew Mom had only convinced herself Jack wasn't going because she couldn't deal with the danger. "Not bad. Fernando will walk to the mountain with me." Jack spoke so softly he barely heard his own voice.

Mom sat down across from Dad, cut off a serving of beef then dipped out Greenthumb Acres potatoes, onions, carrots, and peas. She set the plate down in front of Dad and waved her hand to Fernando. "Join us."

He pulled up a chair and everyone bowed their heads while Dad said grace. Afterward Fernando crossed himself. "If God is for us, who can be against us? Romans 8: 31."

Fernando's quote from the Bible rang in Jack's head as he ate what he could of dinner. He held the words in his heart.

Mom got up, set an apple pie on the table then took her seat again. She slid the dessert to her as though she intended to cut it, but held the knife in mid-air. "I've spoken with Gwenie's parents. They've been at the police station ever since they went to the hospital and found her missing from her room. I'm sure they've convinced the police to hunt for her. When Jack tells Captain Jones Gwenie's on that mountain, they'll have her down in no time."

Jack lowered his head. There'd be no call until he had Gwenie safe in his arms.

Mom cut the pie. "Thank goodness for that stem."

Chapter Fourteen - The Climb

Jack jumped at the sound of the alarm blasting in his ear and switched on the lamp beside his four-poster mahogany bed. Two o'clock. He swung his legs out from under the brown and beige comforter, got up, and straightened it. Confidence and adrenalin pumped through his veins as he caught sight of the first-place trophies for rock climbing on the chest in his room.

He grabbed his breathable, water and windproof trousers and jacket from the walk-in closet and tugged them on. What a fool he'd been to believe Derick's Down-Home Dining was a legitimate restaurant. Maybe the Lord would straighten out the mess he'd made. *Oh please, God.*

If only the beanstalk had grown to the top of the mountain, and he could leave now undetected in the dark. He grabbed the backpack he'd already filled with his gear and the items Fernando picked up for Gwenie. He tip-toed downstairs, walked softly to the front door, and went outside.

Fernando took a step toward him. "There you are. You ready?" he whispered.

"More than."

Fernando turned on a bright flashlight and led Jack across the grassy yard, the beam shining two feet ahead of them in the dark. Crickets chirped and leaves rustled along the sides of their path as they walked into the forest, the light bouncing off a tree as a possum scurried underneath a mountain laurel bush. A fox with a snake in its mouth slinked across a log where a raccoon with bluish gray fur and huge round masked eyes stared at them.

"It's okay. Ignore him." Fernando took another step, and the small, pretty, but potentially rabid creature, ran away.

In fifteen minutes they'd cleared the bridge and forest. They stepped onto the mountain's bottomland, the stars overhead twinkling like diamonds.

Fernando touched the beanstalk. "Looks good. I can't see all the way up, but I think it's safe to go. I sawed the stalk off flat, so you'll know when you get to the top." His dark eyes softened on the corners. "I guess I'll turn this over to you. Should I come back and bring a first aid kit and the law, or what should I do?"

"I'll call if we need any of those things. If you don't hear from me, we're fine. Clearly, the police need to clean up this bunch of gangsters, but they're already on the case, I'm sure. Dad and I, as well as you and Mr. Kasey have talked to them."

Jack lowered his head. "And Gwenie's parents are at the station. As soon as she's safe, we'll tell them about the shack."

Fernando patted Jack's arm. "Do you need the flashlight? I know these woods well. I can get along without it."

"No, I have the headlamp on my helmet and a little starlight from the Heavens. That ought to be enough. So much of climbing is feeling."

"Okay, time's wastin,' good luck, Mister Jack. I'll call the cops if you and Gwenie aren't here by morning." Fernando's eyes grew misty. He blinked then turned and sat down on a log.

Lonely darkness fell around Jack as he slipped into his harness and put on his climbing shoes. He crept in and out of the moon's shadows to the base of the alp and took hold of the strong plant, the itchy touch of it not a problem, the strength of it boosting his confidence. Fueled by the fire burning in his heart to find Gwenie, he stepped on the first node and glanced back. Just one quick look. He didn't know why. Maybe something in his psyche wanted to see the ground from whence he'd come one last time in case he never set foot on it again.

He climbed up the next nodule and the next as fast as his feet and arms would take him. A sense of leaving the everyday world overwhelmed him as it always did when he climbed, but this time it wasn't freeing. An eerie sensation sent shivers through his bones with every foot he scaled. The breaking of twigs, crunching of leaves, and howling

noises below grew fainter and fainter as he
ascended higher and higher.

"Whooo-whoo." Halfway up he met an owl
that turned its head in a circle as it sat on the highest
limb of a towering oak. He pulled upward while
pushing with his lower body as he passed boulders
and scraggly bushes lit by the stars and moon. He
searched with his right hand for the next node,
found it, moved up and placed his foot on the spot
where it had been. The jagged surface on this
mountain could rip open a person in an instant, but
it was Jack's fear for Gwenie that gripped him. The
yearning to hold her safe in his arms seeped deeper
into his pores each time he forged upward.

His body ached as he pulled with nerves
wound as tight as a corkscrew for wanting to hurry
to the top. Soon his leg muscles cramped. A gray
piece of granite jutting out like the seat of a chair
with a slab for a back tempted him. How could he
rest after what he'd done to Gwenie? He had to
keep moving, but what if his arms and legs gave
out, and he never reached her? His head throbbed
with decision making.

Just for a second he let go of the living pole.
His foot slipped, and he slid down the precipice,
debris rolling, crashing beneath him until the belay
caught the rope and stopped his fall. His head swam
as he thrust the spring-loaded camming device into
a crack and anchored the cable. He swung to his
right and sank to the rocky seat. The stones settled

below him and silence filled the darkness where he sat tucked out of the light from Heaven.

Two days ago he was a slap-happy player in love with Gwenie since childhood, but content to drink life's single pleasures a while longer. Now the need to take hold of a more profound passion that seemed as fragile as one of Dad's orchids burned in his soul. The breeze whipping around him blew away images of fast rides through Fairwilde with a blond or a brunette laughing beside him. He needed Gwenie. *Please Lord, let her be alright waiting for me.*

He stretched out his legs then rubbed his palms together. Upward.

He swung out, grabbed hold of the beanstalk, pulled up with his hand and pushed with his foot as a blast of strong wind swayed the sturdy stem. The stars grew dim then disappeared as clouds rolled over them. Raindrops hit his head while lightning flashed, lighting up the sky— nothing but dark space as far as he could see. Then the flash.

He pulled up with his hand and pushed with his right foot—pulled up with his hand and pushed with his right foot again and again through the black void cut by occasional lightning. The tiny glow from the lamp on his helmet did little good in this storm. Another burst of air whipped around him, and the plant quivered. He touched a flat spot. The one Fernando told him to look for? He moved his fingers around it.

Yes. Relief as strong as the gust that bent the trees swept over him. The top. He wanted to shout *I'm here Gwenie!* into the stormy night over and over, but instead he leaned forward trying to see a way into the cabin.

The big vegetable shifted as a lightning bolt split the sky, illuminating the shack five feet away. He grabbed the edge of a huge boulder sticking out from under the house's foundation and crawled onto it. Water rolled off the big stone as he took hold of a tree and hoisted himself into the yard. His heart pounded as he crept to the window, puddles squashing underneath the soles of his shoes. He pressed his face to the glass and peered through the sheet of rain sliding down it. Gwenie sat on an old sofa. In his head he roared as loud as a lion as he lifted the sash.

Rumbling that sounded like an old car idling wafted out.

Jack's cam clanged as it hit the sill. He froze then held it close to him with one hand as he wriggled his way inside and dropped on all fours.

Puffs of air from the big man's snoring blew the pages of the magazines on the rickety coffee table.

Gwenie gasped and rose from the gray sofa. "Shhh." She put her fingers over her lips. Then she rushed to Jack, flung her arms around his neck, and kissed him over and over on his checks.

Finally, she let go and Jack stood. He stroked her cheek, pulled her close, and let his lips wander to hers in a long, deep kiss. He never wanted to let go.

The sleeping giant snorted.

Jack jumped and let go of Gwenie. "We need to go. I brought some things for you to put on."

She touched his shoulder, tears in her eyes. "I can't believe you're here."

Gwenie's captor's large arms flinched.

Urgency pumped through Jack's veins. "We need to hurry."

"I knew you'd come for me. When I saw the lanky, muscular arm moving in the window, I knew it was you." Tears rolled down Gwenie's cheeks.

Jack wiped them away with his thumb. "It's all right. I'm going to take you—"

The kidnapper snorted.

Gwenie and Jack stood still, quiet as statues.

The brute slumped in his seat as Jack unzipped the backpack.

"Quick, put this stuff on." Jack handed Gwenie the mountain climbing shoes and gloves.

Her green eyes grew big. "I've looked out the window. You know I'm scared of heights. I can't go down that cliff."

"You won't have to scale the mountain. You can go down using a beanstalk. It'll be like walking down the stairs backward. I'm going to pull it inside the cabin and hold it for you. All you have to do is step on the first node." Jack tried to put on a cheerful grin. "I'll be with you all the way."

He leaned out the opening, stretching as far as he could. A stiff breeze blew the vegetable out of his reach. His feet hit the floor with a thud when he slid back into the room. "Missed it. I gotta' try again."

The sleeping giant blew out his mouth, and an entire magazine flew onto the floor. The walrus of a man jumped, his eyes open wide like pieces of coal shining in the glow of the lamp beside the tattered over-sized chair.

Chapter Fifteen - The Escape

Gwenie screamed as Jack pulled her close by his side, their bodies against the opened window.

Noble bounded out of his seat and the walls vibrated. "What do you think you're doin', squirt?"

"I'm taking Gwenie out of here."

That dark look came in Noble's eyes. "She can't leave."

"Yes, she can. I'm taking her, and you can't stop me." Jack's voice shook.

Gwenie shivered as she darted looks at Noble then Jack. Would Noble hit Jack?

"Course I can..." Noble got a puppy dog face. "But I don't like hurting people."

Hope trickled into Gwenie's tight muscles.

Jack's stance stiffened. "Stay out of the way."

"You ain't leavin'." Noble pointed at the gray couch. "Get over there."

Gwenie pulled back from Jack. "Once you know Noble you realize he's very nice."

Jack blinked then stared at Gwenie with questioning eyes.

She nodded, trying to tell Jack to go along with the conversation.

Jack knitted his eyebrows. "Where'd you get that name?"

"My mother."

Gwenie gestured with her palm. "He got in the wrong group at school and ended up in Rochester, but he can change his ways."

"Huh?" Noble tilted his head. "Why would I do that?"

Gwenie's mind raced. What did Noble want to hear? "Because you have a good heart. If you keep hanging out with those criminals, you're going to end up in a place much worse than Rochester. You're going to the dungeons."

Noble's eyebrows shot up. "I met a man once who'd stayed there for twenty years."

A twinge of hope pricked Gwenie's heart. Maybe Noble really would like a better life. "That's not what you want."

"But I only have friends in Rochester." Sadness lined Noble's voice. "Nobody else likes me."

Gwenie patted his arm. "I do."

Jack glanced at Gwenie then Noble.

Gwenie locked eyes with Jack. Surely he knew she wanted him to encourage Noble. *Come on, Jack, say something.*

"That's a start." Cheerfulness rang in Jack's tone as though the conversation had made him bolder.

"How about you, squirt? You wanna be friends?"

"If you let me." Jack peered at Noble with steady eyes.

"Let you. What do you mean by that? I ain't stoppin' you." An angry tone scraped through Noble's words, and Gwenie's pulse quickened.

"There are certain things you'd need to do." Jack answered as though he wanted the opportunity to direct Noble.

"Naw, I don't want to be nobody but myself."

Thunder roared outside, lightning flashed across the sky, and the lamp flickered.

Noble snorted. "Sit on that sofa, *now*." He shoved Gwenie onto it.

Jack plopped down beside her and put his arm around her.

She wasn't ready to give up on Noble or leaving the shack. "You don't have to change who you are. You just grow and become a better person."

Noble scratched his head while Jack glanced at the window as though he thought he and Gwenie could leap through it. Silly.

"I don't need to grow. I'm big enough." Noble stared at Gwenie with questioning eyes.

Jack pulled her closer.

"I meant mature," she said.

"Ain't that the same as changing?"

"Not exactly. It's kinda like having cake."

Jack lifted his eyebrows and stared at Gwenie.

"What?" Noble put his hand to his large ear and pulled it forward. "I'm listening."

"Okay, cake's good, but you make it better when you put frosting on the top. If you serve it with ice cream, it's delicious. You haven't altered the cake." Gwenie talked as fast as she could. The sooner Noble became agreeable the better.

Noble guffawed, the rickety coffee table and lamp beside the sofa shaking. "You want me to put frosting and ice cream on my head?"

"Of course not, I'm trying to explain how you can make something better without changing it."

Noble bit his bottom lip while staring at Jack and Gwenie. "What would you suggest I do?"

"Shave." Jack blurted out the word. "The people of Fairwilde would like you much better if you shave."

Gwenie knitted her eyebrows and glared at Jack. She couldn't believe he criticized Noble when she was trying to gain his confidence. "That may be true, but if you're attractive on the inside, they don't really care what's on the outside."

"Naw, you're confusing me. You ain't makin' any sense. I'm gonna' tie up both of you. I don't like the way squirt's lookin' at the window. I told you, I ain't stupid."

"No. We don't think you are. Do we, Jack?"

Jack shook his head.

"If you only listen to me, you can have a better life. You won't ever have to hurt anyone, and people will be kind to you."

Noble got a faraway look in his eyes. "How you gonna' make 'em do that?"

"I'm not. You are. First thing, you come back with us—"

"Whoa." Jack snapped at Gwenie.

"You don't want me?" Noble growled.

Thunder rolled. Lightning lit up the sky. The beanstalk swayed away from the window.

"It's not that. I don't know if that thing—'' Jack nodded toward the beanstalk. " —will hold all three of us, but you could come down after us. We'd wait for you." Jack rushed his words as though he tried to get himself out of a jam.

The giant stomped to the opening, took hold of the living pole, and pulled it inside. "This?"

Gwenie nodded. Noble probably had no idea what a favor he'd just done for Jack and her. "I'm serious. If you want to turn your life around, we're with you."

"What'll you do?"

"All right, if you'll be quiet, I'll tell you exactly what *you* need to do, and how we can assist." Gwenie peered at Jack, trying to use her eyes to communicate that she wanted him to help.

Then she directed her gaze at Noble and motioned toward his chair as she strained her brain for ideas.

Noble dropped down into his seat.

Gwenie's skin tingled with the hope she might turn this situation around if she handled Noble carefully. She took a deep breath. "Don't interrupt."

Noble looked like a kid who'd stolen a cookie. "I promise."

Jack pulled back his shoulders. "First, we'll call my dad and ask if you can come to work for him if you tell the police where to find the guys who destroyed the farm."

Noble opened his mouth, but Gwenie glared at him. "Second, we'll call law enforcement for you, so you can give them the evidence. I won't press charges against you for kidnapping me, so you can go home."

"I don't have a home in Fairwilde."

Thoughts flew fast and furious in Gwenie's head as she tried to bring Noble around. She cut her gaze at Jack. "He built Derick's Down-Home Dining. Did you see the workmanship?"

Jack nodded. "While you're re-building structures on the farm, you can fix up a little apartment out near the hot houses."

Noble smiled. "What can I put in it?"

Jack's blue eyes widened. "The usual stuff, furniture, dishes, knick-knacks, and you can personalize it too. Dad will pay you to work, so you'll have money to spend."

"What about friends?

Relief seeped into Gwenie's pores. It was working. She pointed to herself then Jack. "Start with us."

"I dunno. They're supposed to come back in a helicopter and get Gwenie as soon as Jack's dad signs the farm over to them."

Weakness fell over Gwenie like rain. "And take me where? Do what to me?"

"I dunno where they'll take you, but they promised they wouldn't hurt you."

Wrinkles creased Jack's brow. "My father will never sign the farm over to them."

"Then, I have to kill you."

Gwenie's heart beat so fast she could hardly breathe. "Don't you see? They're going to kill us either way, and they might kill you too."

Thunder rocked the walls.

Noble sat up straight. "I'm too big."

"Not for a machine gun or grenades," Jack said. "Think about our offer. We can help. Eventually, you can go to church with us and find great friends in Fairwilde."

"All right, call your dad. I wanna' go down the beanstalk."

Gwenie relaxed like a balloon with air sifting out of it.

Jack pulled his cell out of his backpack and punched in the number. "Dad, I'm with Gwenie and a man named Noble from Derick's Down-Home Dining."

"Thank God you're safe. You are, aren't you?"

"Yes. Noble wants to know if he can work for you if he tells the police about the men who wrecked the farm."

"Yes, son, anything, let me talk to him."

"Okay." Jack handed the phone to Noble. "He wants to tell you something."

Noble put it to his ear. "All right, you're sure you want to hire me. What? Jack said I could live on your land." Silence. "If you promise, we're coming."

Noble handed the phone to Jack. "Hang up. Let's go."

"Bye Dad. No time to talk. See you." He put his iPhone in his shirt pocket. "Gwenie and I will go first. As soon as you can no longer see us, come down. All you have to do is step from one node to the next."

Gwenie slipped into the harness as Jack handed Noble a rope.

"Here, I brought this for Gwenie, but I can look out for her."

Noble's eyes grew misty as he reached out and took it.

Jack helped Gwenie to the window as the Heavens opened up again with thunder, lightning and pouring rain.

Chapter Sixteen - The Perilous Descent

Gwenie shuddered at the black world outside the window. Jack picked up a flashlight lying on a chest and shined it on the beanstalk. Suddenly the inside of the shack looked safer than the huge plant with water running over every inch of it. "I can't do it."

"Yes, you can. I believe in you. I'll be right in front of you all the way. We'll be so close you can touch my hand."

"All right."

"Put on these gloves."

Someone had gone to some trouble to make her rescue safe. "Where'd you get them?" Gwenie asked as Jack stuck them out to her. Would they keep her hands from slipping?

"Fernando picked them up for you in town." She took them, and he stepped onto the strong stem.

She peered down at him. He looked safe and confident, but he was a champion climber.

"Wrap one leg around each side and hold on tight," he called up to her.

"I'm dizzy."

"Concentrate on sliding one foot down until it touches a nodule. You'll be fine as long as you don't let go. Even if your foot slips, don't panic. I'm right underneath you."

Jack chuckled as though he tried to lighten the mood, but it didn't shake off the fear covering Gwenie like a shroud. In spite of the horror jarring her nerves she knew she had to leave the shack. Jack was so brave to come for her. In a flash of lightning she slid her small foot out the window and stepped on the first node. "These rubber shoes are great. Thanks for bringing them." How could a pair of gloves and shoes make up for her lack of rock climbing experience?

"You're welcome. You'll be fine. We'll be down in no time."

Thunder roared and lightning split the darkness. Gwenie glanced at the jagged rocks beneath her. Her hands froze to the stalk as silent screams resounded in her head. She looked at Jack. His wide eyes beckoned to her. Visions of the two of them walking arm in arm by the river flashed in her mind. Her love for him pulsed through her veins and she loosened her grip. She followed him placing her foot on the next bud then the next again and again.

"I don't see you. I'm coming down." Noble's voice boomed out.

"Wait. We aren't quite to the bottom." Jack yelled upward into the night.

The living pole shook. Gwenie's foot slipped and her body flew out to the side. She screamed then wrapped her arms around the stem, pressing her body against it like glue.

"Don't let go. I'm coming."

The shaking stopped as Jack climbed up and reached his hand out to her. "Take hold."

Gwenie focused on Jack's opened palm and the strength she saw in it. She could trust him. She loved him. She let go with her right hand.

The vibration commenced again.

Gwenie's fingertips missed Jack's and the tremor shook her other hand loose.

Falling, faster and faster, panic filling every bone in her body, she flung her arms. Her heart raced as she sank into darkness. Panting, she flapped her limbs harder and harder, but she plunged down, down, down dropping below Jack. She was going to die.

**

Terror jarred every nerve in Jack's body as adrenalin rushed through him. He clutched a boulder jutting out from the mountain, placed the bottoms of his feet against the beanstalk, and bowed it with a powerful force he didn't know he had. "Grab it. Grab it now."

Gwenie's foot caught on a bud beneath him, and she grasped the stem as the trembling started once more.

Rage toward Noble raced up Jack's spine. "Noble, stooop. We're all going to die," he screamed as loud as he could, but he had to stay calm. He tied the rope around his harness with a shaky hand, uncoiled it, and slid it to Gwenie.

Noble shook the plant and slung the cord out of her grasp.

Jack's blood boiled. First the big ox kidnapped Gwenie. Now he was about to kill both of them. "Noble, be still, or I'm going to put you in jail and let you rot."

His loud plea dissipated into the thunder. He gritted his teeth and swallowed his anger. Gwenie's safety came first. He couldn't lose her. *Oh dear, Lord, please help us.*

Finally, the strong vegetable stilled, and Jack let the line down to her. "You're all right." His insides turned to mush when he thought of the mess he'd made of their lives. "I'm sorry I didn't put this on us to start with. I just wanted to get out of there. I had no idea the brute would get on and nearly knock us off."

Lightning split the sky, illuminating Gwenie pressed against the beanstalk, water running down her cheeks over strands of hair stuck to it. If only he could trade places with her. "Trust me. You're all right."

"I do trust you." She put her feet on two bulges one on either side of the living pole and leaned into it while she held on with one hand.

Hope tingled over Jack. If Noble would just stop rocking them. "You're going to tie a bowline knot around the metal ring on your harness. It's similar to securing thread. First with your free hand pull the cord through and leave a short end."

"Got it."

A twinge of relief relaxed Jack's tense muscles. "All right. Hold the side you're not knotting with your thumb. Use your fingers to bring the short end through." *Lord, please let her do it.*

"I have it."

Thankfulness fell over Jack like the rain pouring on his head. "Good. Now slip your hand out and pull the rope tight."

"All right. I'm doing it. Give me a minute."

Thunder rolled and lightning popped. He had to get Gwenie on the ground. "We're almost at the bottom. As soon as you're ready slide your foot to the next node. If you miss one, I'll pull you up with me."

"Okay. Here I go." Gwenie stepped on the nodule beneath her then another and another until at last she touched the ground.

Jack plopped down right behind her, stretched out on the underbrush and took the first good gulp of air he'd had since they left the shack. Raindrops hit his cheeks and rolled off as Gwenie stumbled and fell on top of him. She clung to him like plastic wrap. He brushed the wet auburn hair and water from her face and kissed her while holding her shivering body. Love and thankfulness for her life filled him as he held her closer and closer trying to bring her nearer to keep her safe. "You're so brave," he whispered.

Fernando appeared out of sheets of rain, carrying a blanket, an umbrella, and a thermos. He helped Jack and Gwenie up and wrapped the covering around Gwenie.

Jack wanted to keep her where he could touch her. He put his arm around her shoulder.

"You're going to catch your death." Fernando poured coffee from the thermos into plastic cups and handed them to Jack and Gwenie. "Here, drink this underneath the oak tree. It will shelter you."

Noble's feet hit the ground with a thud. Water shot up in two-foot splatters.

Fernando's eyes widened.

Jack said, "This is Gwenie's friend, Noble. Noble, Fernando."

The two men nodded.

Jack opened his mouth to ask Noble why he didn't wait for them to get down.

Noble apparently anticipated the question. He cupped his large hand around his ear. "Listen. It's them. That's their helicopter." He sounded frightened.

Jack's mouth gaped. "No one in their right mind would fly in this weather." He didn't hear the aircraft, but he had Gwenie. He didn't care what those creeps did to themselves.

A noise like an egg-beater cut through the pouring rain. It grew louder. A whirr whined. Now he heard it in the distance.

Noble took hold of the beanstalk. "They'll come down as soon as they see this growing in the window." He glanced at Jack. "You got an ax in your backpack?" Determination lined his voice.

Washed out from climbing up the plant and bringing Gwenie down, Jack was numb inside and didn't see the danger. "Yes, but that thing's as strong as steel."

"Give it here," Noble demanded.

Jack doubted Noble could tumble the sturdy plant, but he pulled out the tool. "Here ya' go."

Noble grabbed the ax, slung back his arm and swung. The huge vegetable wiggled. They all lowered their heads and peered at the place where Noble had struck.

Fernando rose and placed his hands on his hips. "You nicked it. Try again."

Noble sucked in air, snorted, and hacked with so much force rain droplets splattered off his arm. *Ka-wham*. The stalk wobbled.

They all bent down and examined it.

The helicopter's blades cutting through the night grew closer. Coming down the mountain hadn't guaranteed safety, even in this desolate forest. Having their escape mechanism intact would point the criminals in their direction. The noise of the copter whirled inside Jack's head, jarring his nerves, alerting him to the impending danger. He focused on Noble. "You're getting it. You're getting it."

Thunder roared. Lightning streaked the sky and lit up the copter flying toward the top of the mountain.

Gwendolyn jumped up and down. "Hurry."

Noble pulled back his arm then pounded the beanstalk again and again. It jiggled with each stroke.

"Don't stop. Keep going. Keep going," Fernando yelled above the thunder. Then he grabbed a hatchet from his bag and whacked the stalk on the other side in the same area. "I'm no giant, but I'll help."

Jack took hold of the plant above the nick where Noble and Fernando pounded and pushed as hard as he could, driving the strong vegetable toward the ground. Gwenie joined him, and soon the beanstalk leaned.

The whirr grew deafening.

They stopped chopping and stared at the sky.

Jack put his hands above his eyes to shield them from the rain. His pulse quickened as angst raced through his veins. "I think it's right over us."

"That's all right. They can't see us in this thunderstorm." Fernando wiped his palms on his pants' legs.

"As long as the lightning holds off until they fly past us, we should remain stay to them," Gwenie said.

"It's a wonder they don't crash in this weather." Jack rubbed his forehead.

"They're too mean to wreck. We need to get this thing down before they see it." Noble swung the ax so fast the blade blurred again and again. Fernando chopped, and Jack and Gwenie pushed.

Finally the stalk separated at the cut, but the top portion slipped over the bottom and stood upright. Noble grasped it and yanked. He grunted, wiped water from his eyes and jerked again...again...and again.

Jack, Fernando, and Gwenie took hold of the portion sticking out from behind him, the whirr above them deafening.

Lightning flashed.

"Pull harder. They're almost there. We gotta' get the top of the stalk away *now.*" Noble dragged it and groaned. He snorted and repeated his action. Jack, Fernando and Gwenie heaved each time he grunted. At last the stalk lay on the ground.

Noble rested a minute, taking deep breaths. "We're safe from the machine guns and grenades. They'll never know a large beanstalk was there." Noble chortled. Then his laughter boomed into the night. "They'll think we flew out the window." He grabbed his stomach and bent over as Fernando snickered. Gwenie and Jack laughed too.

Gwenie hugged him, water squishing from his black shirt. "Thank you."

Jack and Fernando shook his hand. Then Fernando put one arm around Gwenie's shoulder and one over Jack's. "They're waiting for us. Let's go home. Come on, Noble."

"What they gonna' say when they see the likes of me?"

"They're going to say, 'Nice to meet you, Noble,'" Gwenie said.

Jack, Noble, Fernando, and Gwenie splashed through the dark forest, twigs snapping beneath their shoes as rain splattered on the ground. Jack walked with his arm around Gwenie's waist, holding her tight. He couldn't wait to relax with just her and him. Oh, the things he wanted to tell her.

Chapter Seventeen - Noble Meets the Family

Jack squinted as he led the group across the yard, the white plantation home in the distance barely visible in the rain. Steel gray lightened the dark sky as if someone slowly lifted a shade to daybreak while they followed him to the porch. They trudged up the steps, Noble's footfalls thumping on the planks.

Bertille swung open the door, took one look at Noble standing underneath the soft glow of the porch light, and gasped.

He lowered his head.

Jack let go of Gwenie and swung his hand toward him. "Bertille, this is Noble. He saved our lives."

Bertille stuck out her chubby right hand. "Thank you." She directed her gaze at Jack. "Your mama and daddy are in the kitchen. I have the biggest pan of scrambled eggs, bacon, and homemade biscuits. There's a fresh pot of coffee and pecan sweet rolls." Bertille looked up at Noble. "I figured after being on the mountain, and then coming down at night in a thunderstorm, you'd be cold."

Gwenie rubbed her arms and directed her gaze at Bertille. "You're right. I wonder if it's ever summer up there."

"I'll take you to the kitchen then get dry clothes." Her eyes moved from Noble's head to his toes. "Don't you worry, Mr. Noble. I think we got some pants around here big enough in the waist." She bit her lip. "They might be a little short."

They followed Bertille.

Jack's mom and dad sprang from their straight-back chairs at the big round oak table and hugged Jack and Gwenie.

Dad offered his hand to Noble. "Thank you for bringing them back. I'm Fred Greenthumb."

He shook it. "Noble."

"Oh yes. I was so afraid for Jack to go. I begged him not to go, but I knew he was...." Mom's voice trailed off, and her eyes grew misty. She grabbed Noble around the neck and hugged him.

A twinge of guilt pricked Jack's skin, but he knew he'd done the right thing, and deep down he realized Mom knew it too.

Noble patted Mom on the back until she let go.

Dad motioned to a chair. "Have a seat. I'm sure all of you are starving."

Bertille wandered in carrying the clothes for Gwenie and Noble in her arms.

Fred gestured with his palm. "Go ahead and change before we eat."

"Miss Gwendolyn will go in the guest bathroom, and Mr. Noble can use the den." Bertille handed them the clothes.

Gwenie held out her hand to Noble. "I need to call my mom and dad."

Noble lowered his head as though in guilt, reached in his shirt pocket and pulled out a cell phone. "Sorry, here. I didn't hurt it, and it's still in the plastic waterproof case."

"No problem. We're all safe. That's what matters." Gwenie took it and left.

Jack dashed to his room. He couldn't get off his rainproof pants and jacket fast enough. Even they hadn't stayed dry in the deluge as long as he'd been in it. Poor Gwenie must have been chilled to the bone. He tugged on a pair of jeans with the knot of fear he'd had for his and her life still coiled in his stomach. All the love he had for her overflowed and made his heart swell. What an idiot he'd been to fall for the trap Noble had set at George's garage. He yanked on a tee shirt and returned to the kitchen.

Noble wore pants, that just as Bertille had said, looked like knickers. He looked like gelatin protruding at the seams in a one-size-fits all navy tee shirt Jack had won in a rock climbing competition.

Mom's green sheath sundress showed off Gwendolyn's petite, curvy body.

Jack couldn't stop staring at her and couldn't stop the shame crawling all over his skin for the tragedy he'd caused. Could he ever forgive himself?

They pulled their chairs to the table, scraping them across the gray laminate floor as Bertille set down a large bowl of grits.

Fred motioned toward an empty seat. "Join us. Let's all bow our heads."

Bertille sat down and folded her hands in her lap while Dad said grace. Afterward he picked up the plate of bacon while Mom sent around a platter of sweet rolls. The breakfast aromas tickled Jack's nose as he plopped a big dollop of butter on his toast.

Mom directed her gaze at Gwenie. "Would your parents like to join us? How are they?"

Gwenie sighed. "They're okay. They were still at the police station. They said for me to meet them at the house. No rush. I think they're going to shower and take a nap when they get there."

"I was praying hard for both of you." Dad took a sip of his coffee. "After Jack called and asked if Noble could work for me, I contacted Captain Jones. He'll be here soon, but in the meantime tell us what happened?"

Jack told him about the shack and how the beanstalk grew to the window, and he and Gwenie climbed down, Noble behind them. He swallowed back remorse and disgrace as he remembered Gwenie falling. It was all his fault, the kidnapping and her near death experience.

Fernando described the horrible storm, the helicopter, and Noble chopping down the plant of steel.

Mom's blue eyes grew wider and wider. Bertille's mouth gaped, and Fred sat back in his seat as though spellbound.

"It wasn't all that hard. Why when I wuz five years old, I cut down big trees behind our house for firewood in the winter," Noble chimed in.

Bertille, Mom and Dad exchanged glances as though they didn't approve of a five-year-old splitting wood.

Jack set down his fork. "It was an experience I never want to have again. I'm thankful I'm here having this delicious meal. I'm so sorry I got Gwenie into this." Mere words couldn't describe the agony in his heart.

"It was inevitable. They were coming after me to get to you and your dad. If it hadn't happened like it did, it would have happened some other way." Gwenie directed her gaze from one of them to the other. "Thanks to all of you I'm safe." She gave a tired smile.

Jack's tense muscles relaxed. Right now his part in this disaster strangled so much life out of him he hardly could breathe. He'd probably never stop asking himself how he could have fallen for Noble's trick. But he could see Gwenie's point.

None of them could ever know how things would've gone down if he hadn't. Gratefulness filled him for the forgiveness she'd given him.

Bertille hopped up from her chair. "I'll get more coffee."

In minutes everyone's cups steamed with their refills.

Gwenie picked up hers. "You can't imagine how the thugs pushed around Burly Man, uh, Noble."

Mom and Betille glanced at Noble and giggled. In spite of being riddled with guilt and having nerves still on edge from the climb, Jack couldn't help but chuckle inside. It overflowed. Even Fernando and Dad laughed.

Wrinkles creased Gwenie's brow. "Not physically. He may be big, but he isn't mean like the rest of them."

Noble tilted his head and stared at Gwenie.

"I'll let him tell you about the creeps. Go ahead. You have new friends here."

Noble's voice boomed across the table. "When I was in school, the kids wouldn't have anything to do with me, so I got into the wrong crowd and ended up in Rochester. That's where I met the Crowbars, the gang I'm in—uh, was in."

Fred leaned forward. "Why do they want to buy the farm?"

Noble shook his head. "I dunno. It has somethin' to do with the land value. It's more than just dirt for raising crops."

Fred scratched his head. "What? Do they think there's gold on it? It's only as valuable as the appraisal. I don't understand, but maybe they'll tell us when Captain Jones brings them in. We're going to let him know how much you've helped us. I'll also tell him you're my newest employee. You can start by cleaning the processing plant."

Noble's dark eyes grew misty. "Really, Mr. Greenthumb, you aren't goin' to change your mind?"

"No, we don't do that here. My word's as good as an acre of land."

Jack still wasn't sure Noble could change his ways as quickly as he claimed, but he had to admit, Noble saved their lives, and for that, he wanted to give Noble the chance he'd never gotten in life.

Fred sighed. He took a sip of his coffee and set down the cup. "I wonder what Captain Jones has done. What's taking him so long?"

Chapter Eighteen - The Proposal

The warmth from family and friends, not to mention Gwenie, flowing around the big oak table settled Jack's nerves. The familiar soft down-lighting underneath the pine cabinets glowing on the white counters reminded him of all the meals he'd eaten in safety with his mom and dad. He pushed back his chair, got up, and held his hand out to Gwenie to help her up. "Let's wait outside for Captain Jones."

He grabbed a handful of paper towels from the dispenser on the counter to wipe off the wet seat and escorted Gwenie to the swing on the front porch. Water gurgled in the gutter behind them when they sat down. Sheets of raindrops falling from the roof between the posts looked like rippling glass as it pattered onto the wooden planks.

Jack pulled Gwenie to his chest. "I've never been so scared in my life."

"You should have been in my shoes."

"I wish it had been me. When I went in that empty hospital room, it was like someone yanked out my insides. All I wanted to do was find you. I charged out to nowhere. Finally, it dawned on me, if I went to the cabin I might hear something.

Gwenie looked up at Jack and batted her long lashes. "I knew you'd come for me."

Jack's heart beat faster and faster as he squeezed her tighter and tighter. His head swirled like a Tilt-a-Whirl with visions of Gwenie twirling in his mind. He nibbled along her neck, kissing her cheeks, possessing her lips. He floated amid the clouds, but the sky was not big enough to hold him. "Gwendolyn, Gwendolyn." His mouth said her name over and over, but he wasn't telling it to. The words spewed from somewhere deep inside him, and he couldn't stop them. He pressed his heart next to hers, running his hands through her long silky hair, his lips finding hers again. This was where he wanted to stay for the rest of his life, melding himself to her, becoming one, the two of them floating from the sky to an unknown planet.

He needed to touch her shoulders, her arms, her hands and waist. She was here. She was safe. "I never want us separated again."

Gwenie bolted from his chest. "We can't change our lives because of my kidnapping. We have plans for college."

How could he make Gwenie know what was in his heart? How could he show her he only wanted to be with her? "It isn't because of the kidnapping.

It's because I want to stay with you, protect you, and make sure no one ever hurts you. I couldn't stand to lose you ever. You mean more to me than school—than anything."

"Except the little red car." Gwenie chuckled.

Of course she'd say that. Until Noble captured Gwenie he'd acted like that vehicle was the most important thing in his life. "I'm going to have that thing repaired, sell it, and never own another red car as long as I live."

Gwenie blinked her eyes. "I believe you're serious."

"Absolutely. Gwenie, please. Say we'll be together forever. I've loved you since first grade."

Gwenie put her arms around Jack and hugged him then she sat back in silence as though she didn't know what to say.

"Will you marry me?" Jack gazed at her with pleading blue eyes. Now she had to believe him. Proposing was the real thing not an afternoon spin in a sports car. "I know it's not a romantic candlelight dinner, and I don't even have a ring. I've been a little busy."

Gwenie hugged him again. "My hero."

"Is that a yes? I promise we'll have a wonderful meal complete with candles and the ring in the box soon."

"As long as we don't eat at Derick's Down-Home Dining."

"You got it."

Wrinkles creased Gwenie's brow. "What about college?"

Her expression scraped Jack's skin like sandpaper. He thought she'd be elated and thinking only of how much she loved him. But of course, he'd come up with a plan, and she hadn't. "In between snooping at the cabin, climbing up the mountain, and befriending Noble I've thought about that."

Gwenie laughed.

"Even though Wonder State's noted for agriculture and business, Create U may have enough courses in those subjects for me to go there, or you could check out Wonder for their classes. We still have time to switch schools if we get it set up in the next week."

Gwenie nodded. "Yes, we'll do that. When should we get married?"

"Before August."

"That doesn't give me much time to get ready."

"I'll help. Aren't the ceremonies pretty much the same at the chapel of Happy Endings / New Beginnings?"

"All weddings come with their own challenges." Gwenie smiled. "But it'll be fun overcoming them. I'll call the staff tomorrow and reserve our place." Gwendolyn leaned back in the swing and pushed hard with her feet. "Wheee! I'm marrying Jack."

Jack pushed too. They flew almost to the rooftop, nearly conked Captain Jones on the head as he stepped onto the porch.

"Slow down." Gwenie dragged her feet.

Jack did too. They stopped, got up, and joined Captain Jones.

"Sorry, we nearly hit you," Jack said, his steps so light he could have floated.

"I'm glad you missed. It's good to see you on this porch swinging rather than at the hospital."

Jack opened the door. "No kidding. We've got a story you're not going to believe. And..." Jack emphasized the word and. "...we have someone to tell us what we don't know."

Within seconds they strolled into the kitchen. Fernando, Dad, Mom, and Noble sat at the round oak table.

Mom ran her finger around the edge of a light blue placemat. "I can't believe Jack, Gwenie, and Noble came down the mountain in this pouring rain."

"There must have been an angel with us," Noble said.

Dad glanced at Captain Jones. "Come in. Have a seat. Would you like a cup of coffee?"

"Yes, thank you." Captain Jones sat as Gwenie and Jack pulled up a chair. If he was surprised to see Noble, he didn't show it.

Mom got up and served him.

He took a sip of his drink then pulled a notepad from his back pocket. "After seeing the hot houses and the plant today I called in Crime Investigators."

Fernando put his hand over his mouth. "I touched some of the flowers. I guess I shouldn't have, but the stems needed to be repaired soon to save them."

Captain Jones pulled his blond eyebrows together. "You didn't clean up the debris, did you?"

"No."

"I understand. I think we can wrap this up without disturbing them. So..." Captain Jones rubbed his palms together. "What happened?"

Jack told Captain Jones about the kidnapping, and Noble's huge shoulders slumped. He sat as quiet as dew on morning grass.

Captain Jones scratched his head. "You say they're holed up in that old shack on top of the mountain?"

Noble propped his elbows on the table and it wobbled. "Sorry. Yes. They're probably there now, but when they notice the open window, they'll start nosing around until they find out why."

"Let's go over your part in this again, Mr. Noble." Captain Jones gave Noble a steady stare.

Gwenie held up her hand in "stop" fashion. "I'm not pressing charges. He saved our lives."

Jack still wasn't one-hundred percent sure Gwenie should trust Noble as much as she did, but she was a good judge of character. And it was true, he had saved their lives. He deserved a chance.

"That's your right ma'am, but his testimony could help us lock up these guys for a long time." He nodded toward Noble. "Start at the beginning."

Noble snorted and cleared his throat. "I went to live in Rochester while I was in high school."

"I don't think you need to go that far back." Jack elbowed Noble's arm. "Just start when you met the criminals."

Wrinkles creased Noble's brow. He shook his head the way people do when they hate something happened. "I was working in Pete's garage last year, washing and waxing cars after they'd been serviced. One day two men came over to me as I was polishing a windshield. One of 'em had red hair, blue eyes, and a scar across his face. He's the one who started talking to me. He says, 'We have mutual friends, Fancy Frogs and Tim Berkowitz. They said you were strong. You look it. Are you?'

"That mark on his face looked pretty nasty, so I start wonderin' if he wants to fight. I shuffled over to a wooden table in the garage where we set things, picked up a soda can, and mashed the air out of it. His eyes bulged. 'You're the man we need,' he said. I asked him, 'What do you want me for.' He asks, 'You wanna make five thousand dollars?' He had my attention. 'Doing what?' I asked.

"'Not much. We need someone to do heavy lifting.' I tell him, 'Sure, when? The red-head says he'll be in touch."

Captain Jones flipped a page on his notepad. "What happened next?"

"He asked me to carry a safe out of a building at midnight. I thought there was something stinky about that. Later I heard about the East End Mall caper." Noble rubbed the top of his head. "Seems like it ain't a good idea to tell you all this. I don't want no trouble."

"Fred has spoken to the District Attorney about you. You're being offered immunity to testify against Fancy, Tim, and anyone else who's involved in this crime ring."

A big smile spread on Noble's face, his dark eyes twinkling. "He's my friend."

Captain Jones nodded. "I can see that. Well, go on."

Mom stood, picked up the coffee pot, and made her way around the table filling everyone's cups, the aroma of hazelnut wafting through the room.

"I picked up some more heavy stuff—big screen televisions from homes where people were out of town and appliances from houses under construction---all in the middle of the night. I wondered about it, but hey, the money was good, and none of these people ever meant anything to me. I wasn't hurtin' nobody—just linin' my pockets. It hadn't been easy to make a livin' since I didn't graduate from high school. I was all right with it. Then—then—they demanded I get this girl out of the hospital and take her to the shack on the mountain. Tim would fly us there they said. I didn't like the sound of it, but they threatened to turn me in for stealing all that stuff *they* told me to take."

Jack's insides shook inside when Noble started talking about taking Gwenie.

Captain Jones put down his pad and wiggled his long fingers. "I need names, addresses, and phone numbers.

Noble took a deep breath. I dunno addresses, and they don't always call from the same phone. One of 'em goes by Red Head, the other, Frank. There are...uh were... my friends, Fancy Frogs and Tim. That's all I know." He pulled his cell phone out of his pants pocket and handed it to Captain Jones. "Maybe this will help."

Captain Jones shut his notepad and took the cell. "It's a good thing you have immunity. You can't go around breaking and entering and stealing."

Noble hung his head.

"But you have a new start." Captain Jones scratched his chin. "It was a good deal if we catch the masterminds and you follow the straight and narrow. Take advantage of this opportunity and turn your life around."

Noble's eyes widened like those of a scared kid. "I'll do my part."

"The only way to get to the hide-away..." Captain Jones chuckled. "Other than by beanstalk, of course, is in a helicopter. This is confidential information, but I think you've earned the right to know. Tomorrow we'll borrow several military

copters and man them with policemen. We believe
the criminals will think we're part of a training
mission from Fairwilde Air Force. They fly across
the mountain fairly often. We should catch these
criminals by surprise because they won't expect us
to land." Captain Jones stood and pushed in his
chair. "Thank you for the coffee." He directed his
gaze at Noble. "If you could come down tomorrow
and give our sketch artist descriptions, we'd
appreciate it."

"Sure."

Mom and Dad walked to the door with
Captain Jones then returned to the kitchen.

Mom glanced at Gwenie then Jack. "Go
ahead and take Gwenie home to see her parents.
Then I'd love it if the two of you come back here to
unwind this evening instead of going out on the
town."

After all Mom had been through Jack agreed
quickly. "Sure Mom."

"Thank you, I'd like that, Mrs.
Greenthumb," Gwenie said.

Noble stood in the middle of the floor
balling his hands into fists, letting them go, and
repeating the action. "The way those guys tricked
me. The hurt and upset they caused all of you. Do
you think Captain Jones will catch them?"

Chapter Nineteen - The Intruder

Twilight danced on the mimosa blooming outside Jack's bedroom window when he woke from his afternoon nap. He propped up the brown decorative pillow, laid his head on it, and stared at the ceiling. Blessed rest. He savored the safety and warmth of his room, but he couldn't wait to pick up Gwenie. He didn't want to be away from her for a minute. He swung his legs out of bed and marched to the bathroom for a shower.

He suspected Mom had an ulterior motive when she asked Gwenie to come over tonight. She was super-excited about the wedding. He smiled inside as he reached around the shower curtain and grabbed a towel. It would be fun listening to Gwenie and her talk about it.

He whistled as he bounded out of the bathroom and dressed in a pair of jeans and a light blue shirt. Several splashes of woodsy cologne added the final touch. He headed down the oak staircase to the shiny clean kitchen and opened the refrigerator door, the light making a streak across the gray tile floor.

A turkey and cheddar on rye. Thank you, Bertille. He snatched it up, gulped it down, and flew out the backdoor to a Greenthumb Acres van. Most girls probably wouldn't want to ride in it, but judging from Gwenie's comments about the red car, she didn't mind at all.

Within fifteen minutes pebbles crunched underneath the tires as he pulled into her drive, parked, and got out.

Water babbling over the rocks in the Awasai and the dampened earthen smell wafting from the ground sent the peace of nature rippling through Jack as he strolled to Gwenie's door and rang the bell.

"Hi." Her voice sounded cheerful despite all she'd been through.

Jack wanted to take her in his arms and kiss her over and over, but he needed to get back to Greenthumb Acres. He reached over and gave her a peck on the lips. "You look gorgeous." She wore a yellow sundress, her long auburn hair lying over her shoulders.

Her mouth curved into a smile. "You wouldn't know last night and this morning I was drenched to the bone after climbing down a steep mountain, where I'd been held hostage until a handsome man rescued me?"

Jack kissed her lightly on the cheek. "Nope."

He escorted her to the van and headed back home. They arrived at the plantation within twenty minutes and joined Mom and Noble in the den.

Mom knitted lace with her antique tortoise shell needle. The light of day shining in the window beside her chair gave way to twilight. She clicked on the lamp on the occasional table then glanced up. Her lips parted into a smile. "Hey, you two."

Noble waved from his seat on the sofa. "Hullo." His deep voice cut into the room.

Jack and Gwenie sat down beside him. Contentment seeped into Jack's pores as the sound of large fire-powered egg beaters filled the sky.

Noble moved his feet off the ottoman. "Listen. They're going for the bad guys."

Mom clinched a fist. "I hope they get every single one of them."

Noble stood. "Me too. Want anything from the kitchen?"

Mom relaxed her hand. "No, thank you."

Gwenie and Jack peered at him and shook their heads no. Then Noble left.

The window rattled beside Mom. She stopped knitting and turned as it popped open. Like a jack out of a box, a man with thin legs sprang into the room and hopped around.

Mom turned white, her mouth gaping.

Gwenie scrunched against Jack as the man sprang forward, jumping like a frog toward her.

Mom stuck him in his backside with her needle.

He stopped in his tracks, rubbed the spot then yanked on Gwenie's arm. "You're coming with me."

Mom screamed and Gwenie clenched Jack's shirt.

"Let go of her, frogman. I'm only going to warn you once."

The man jumped up and down on spindly legs and made a throaty rib-it noise.

Mom shot out of her chair, wielding her needle like a weapon. "Get out of our house now," she hollered as she jabbed the needle into his leg. He leapt a foot in the air. She pierced his arm and punctured his rear again.

He drew a gun from a holster at his ankle. "Don't move." He took bow-legged steps and stood over Gwenie, the gun hanging in his hand at his side. "You're coming with me," he repeated.

Jack's head swam. What was this crazy man doing here? Why wasn't he at the mountain house with the rest of the criminals? Did they think he was bringing Gwenie back to that God-forsaken shack? Not on his life. He gritted his teeth and took a step toward Fancy Frogs.

Noble walked through the doorway, his eyes widening. He set his steaming cup of coffee on the floor. Slipping around behind Fancy Frogs, he jerked him up by the collar.

Fancy Frogs pointed the gun at Gwenie.

She turned white as the oleander in the green houses.

Noble pushed up Fancy Frog's arm, the gun wiggling as Fancy's hand wobbled. Fear it might go off and fire who knew where rushed up Jack's spine as Fancy Frogs shot a hole in the ceiling.

Gwenie sank into the sofa as Mom gasped.

Jack lunged toward Fancy Frogs as Noble knocked the weapon out of Fancy's hand. It hit the floor with a thud.

Noble glared at Fancy Frogs. "You idiot. You coulda' killed somebody."

Mom walked backward to her chair and plopped down in it, the color drained from her cheeks. "Pfff." She blew out her mouth and fanned her face with her small hand. Then she reached in her sewing bag for her cell phone. "I'm calling Captain Jones right now."

Noble glanced at Jack while holding on tight to Fancy Frogs' arm as he jumped up and down. "Where do you want him?"

"Somewhere we can watch him until the police get here." Jack scanned the room as Fancy Frogs stopped hopping around. "By the door. I'll get a rope."

Jack left and returned with a heavy cord.

Dad walked in and stopped short. I thought I heard someone down here." He peered at Fancy Frogs. "Who are you?'

Fancy Frogs made a guttural sound that resembled "rib-it, rib-it."

"He wants to take Gwenie back with him to that shack. He was holding her at gun point, but

Noble rescued her, and *I've* called Captain Jones. He's on his way." Mom put her phone away.

Dad raised his arm with the cast on it over Fancy Frogs. "Think you're smart, huh? You'll find out better as soon as Captain Jones gets here. You can join your cronies in jail."

Noble pushed Fancy Frogs into a straight-back chair, and he and Jack tied him up. Fancy Frog's red, bloodshot eyes blazed with anger. He smirked at Noble. "You'll be sorry when I don't take Gwendolyn to Tim, and you see what he's going to do to you."

"Next time you see Tim he'll be wearing handcuffs." Jack gazed at Gwenie then shot an angry glare at Fancy. "What do you want with her? That's just evil. She never hurt anybody."

"None of your business." Fancy Frogs sat in the chair, his legs so bowed one draped over the right side of the seat; the other over the left.

Mom rubbed her face as Noble sat in the easy chair, and Dad dropped down onto the recliner. They looked like boxers in their corners between rounds. Jack took his seat beside Gwenie on the sofa. Silence fell over the room as though everyone was too stunned to speak. Fancy Frogs uttered that low throaty noise over and over. Jack's nerves shook like he was in a blender. If only he could think of something to say to cover up the irritating racket.

Finally, Mom leaned forward toward Gwenie. "Are you all right?" Her voice sounded like a whisper amid the rib-its bubbling from Fancy's mouth.

"I am now that I know I'm not going to be kidnapped again."

Mom gazed at Gwenie. "I'm so sorry that happened, and because of us."

Jack pulled Gwenie to his chest. "Nothing's ever going to happen to her again as long as I'm around." He glared at Fancy. "How'd you know Gwenie would be here?"

"Rib-it. Where else would she be? Rib-it. I knew she'd show up sooner or later. It was a matter of peering in the window."

Gwenie snuggled up to Jack and glared at Fancy Frogs. "I'm not afraid with Jack here."

Jack kissed her on the forehead.

"Rib-it, rib-it. You people. I'm gonna throw up."

Mom shook her needle at Fancy. "Don't you dare." She directed her gaze at Gwenie. "Soon we can put this behind us and think about the wedding. I suppose you'll have it at the Happy Endings / New Beginnings Chapel."

"Yes ma'am."

Mom's lips spread into a quivering grin. "You can call me Melisse. They have such a lovely reception hall. I love the chocolate fountain where guests scoot by and add sauce to their pieces of cake, ice cream, or whatever." Sparks of happiness filled her voice as though there were so many inside she couldn't contain them, even after the scare, even with Fancy Frogs thumping his feet. Thank goodness, they had Mom. She'd always given them hope even in the darkest of times. "And the strawberries dipped in chocolate on the fruit tree. I can't wait."

Fancy Frogs licked his mouth with his thin, pointed tongue.

Gwenie slid to the edge of her seat. "What else do you think? How about the Fairy Tale Singers out back—"

"Amid orchids. We can supply all the flowers you want in any color. We'll have plenty by then." Mom's eyes lit up. She'd donated floral sprays to others on many occasions, and for Jack and Gwenie's wedding…well, words probably couldn't describe her generosity.

The doorbell rang.

Jack got up and left. He returned with Captain Jones and pointed at Fancy Frogs. "There he is. Noble captured him, saved us all again. Fancy Frogs had a gun."

Noble handed the weapon to Captain Jones. Then he untied Fancy Frogs and Captain Jones handcuffed him. They started toward the front door, but Captain Jones looked over his shoulder at Noble. "If Fred doesn't need you full-time, I think we could use you on the force."

Fred waved at Captain Jones. "I'll share. Maybe he can find out why these creeps wanted my land."

"Yeah, Dad. You been holding back?
What's out there on the farm we don't know about?

Chapter Twenty - Meeting Priscilla

Gwenie's open-back clogs clomped as she walked across the large parking lot to the red brick police station. The sun glinted off the silver and glass entrance as she opened the door.

Inside she passed through the metal detector, stood in the large lobby with folding chairs lined up against two walls, and waited for Jack and his parents.

A woman with a tattoo of a rose on her biceps and a red bandana around her head sat beside the doorway and peered at her lap. Gwenie couldn't help but wonder what trouble had brought her here. *She* certainly didn't want to be here, but Noble had to sign the testimonies he'd given Captain Jones about the crimes of the Crowbars and give the artist descriptions. She and the Greenthumbs promised to be here when he talked to Captain Jones.

Jack entered with Melisse and Fred, and they started toward the seats. Captain Jones and

Noble walked into the large waiting area from a door on the left side of the room. Noble looked spiffy, all shaved and dressed in the jeans and brown shirt Bertille had made for him last night.

Mr. Greenthumb strolled to them. Gwenie, Jack, and Melisse followed. "Did his descriptions help you?" Mr. Greenthumb asked.

Captain Jones smiled big. "Oh yes, come on back."

They marched into a narrow hallway as Captain Jones held the thick, metal door. The click behind them reminded Gwenie that some people here were too mean to associate with the rest of society. A chill ran through her as they went single-file to an office on the right.

Captain Jones motioned for them to sit down. "I had extra chairs brought in for you."

The metal bases clanked as they pulled them up. Sun shining through the slats in blinds on a high window split the black pad on Captain Jones's laminate desk.

He leaned forward. "I wanted to thank you once again for all the help you gave us. I thought you deserved to know first. We've arrested and charged James Rudge and Slippery Cuthbreath with accessory to kidnapping and vandalism. Also, they're wanted in Rochester, along with Fancy Frogs and Tim Berkowitz, for drug trafficking and murder. They hid out in the shack on the mountain, coming down only to eat and gamble at the cabin Slippery's uncle left him. No one had used it in so many years most folks, including me, had forgotten about it. I imagine they counted on that."

Mr. Greenthumb nodded. "How'd the capture go?"

Captain Jones sat back. "Worked like a charm. Apparently, they didn't suspect a thing until the swat team landed armed and ready. By the time they reached for their weapons they were already in the line of fire and had to surrender."

Wrinkles creased Jack's brow. "What were they doing in Fairwilde hanging around Greenthumb Acres? I don't understand why they wanted to buy Dad's farm in the first place, and if they really wanted it, why would they destroy it? And what did Gwenie have to do with any of it?"

Thank you, Jack. Curiosity filled Gwenie as she waited on the edge of her seat for Captain Jones's answer.

He directed his gaze at Jack's dad. "I don't know if you realize it or not, but you've got oil on your land."

Jack's dad sat up straight. "Where?"

"Underneath the hot houses." Captain Jones pulled a piece of paper out of his desk drawer. "One of the gamblers got hold of this map from 1850, showing oil was discovered, but oil drilling wasn't allowed in Fairwilde until the 1960's. That's about the time you moved here from Ireland, settled, started farming, and built the green houses."

Mr. Greenthumb's mouth gaped. "How could this be? There was no information in the survey about oil?"

"Nope. Seems the gambler's dad, who was a gangster too, had gotten hold of the old map and removed it from the courthouse. When he passed away last year, the gambler found it in his dad's belongings."

Jack's mom sucked in air and blew it out. "Wow!"

Jack's eyes widened. "It's all starting to come together, but how'd Slippery and James do so much damage to the farm in one night."

"The gamblers joined them. They're at least twelve of them. If they'd succeeded in getting you to sell, drilled on the property, and had their well come in, there would have been enough oil for all of them to share the riches."

Jack took Gwenie's hand. "They thought if they took Gwenie, I'd convince Dad to sell to get her back. They must have believed no one could even find her, let alone get to her in that shack on Mount Morgan." He nearly whispered the words as though he didn't want to say them or have them be true.

Captain Jones nodded. "You're exactly right."

Noble shook his head. "I'm so dumb."

Fred reached up and patted Noble's huge shoulder. "No. Not at all. You were sent to Rochester as a child, raised in that horrible place with ruthless characters. That's all you knew. Their capers didn't sound any stranger to you than me asking Fernando to stock the hot houses." Fred blinked his eyes. "Legally, of course."

Noble nodded. "That's right, until they told me to take Gwenie, and I wasn't about to hurt her or nobody." His voice trailed off and he looked down as though he couldn't face what he'd done.

Gwenie hoped someday he'd forgive himself. She'd forgiven him. "You didn't hurt anyone. What's more, you saved our lives."

Captain Jones placed his palms on his desk. "I believe Noble's turning his life around for the better, and I was serious about using him from time to time. We'll educate, train, and deputize him for part time."

Noble sat straight up, his dark eyes twinkling. "I'd like that if it's all right with Mr. Greenthumb."

Dad glanced at Noble. "There's no reason he can't start right away working part time for the Fairwilde Police Department. Give me a call, and we'll arrange a schedule."

Captain Jones scooted his chair back from his desk. "Great."

They stood, and Captain Jones offered his hand to Jack's dad. "I hope everything will be up and running soon."

Mr. Greenthumb shook it. "Thank you. We have lots to be thankful for. We've planted the fields with crops we'll harvest in early fall. We're all right. As a matter of fact, Bertille's prepared a little celebration for us."

Captain Jones grinned. "Sounds great. Well, you won't have any more trouble from those creeps. By the way, I'm not telling anyone about the oil. It's your land—your secret, or yours to start drilling."

Gwenie scratched her head. The Greenthumbs already had plenty, but finding the wealth oil could bring sometimes changed people. What if it changed Jack? Her heart fluttered.

Jack turned his head toward his dad. "Don't think we're interested."

Gwenie took a sigh of relief. She loved Jack just as he was.

Mr. Greenthumb tilted his head. "I'll think about it. My life's been spent putting seeds in the ground and growing them into vegetables to eat and flowers to brighten the world." He bit his bottom lip. "Then again, if we could move the greenhouses and put in a rig, we might be able to put more people to work. Maybe, we could help others in Rochester as long as they wanted to stay on a straight and narrow path and were committed to doing it. Of course, we'd have to invent a clean method of drilling, but the folks in Fairwilde are up to it."

Captain Jones escorted them to the waiting room. Then they walked out the door down the wide cement steps.

Jack tapped his dad's arm. "What's Bertille got planned?"

Fred grinned. "You'll see. I'll just say we can't let Noble miss it."

***

The aroma of hazelnut coffee and brownies wafted into the foyer, making Jack's mouth water. The smell grew stronger mesmerizing him by the time he reached the kitchen door. He stopped short.

The biggest girl he'd ever seen stood behind the island with Bertille. Long dark brown curls cascaded to her shoulders. Her eyes danced when she cast her gaze at Noble.

He may have been in Rochester, deprived of the finer things most of his life, but apparently he recognized quality. He shot over to her as though someone had set a firecracker underneath him, as though his heart knew she was there for him. He stuck out his hand. "Noble. How are you?"

"Fine. I'm Priscilla." Her sweet voice, so soft for her size, rang into the room.

Bertille chuckled. "Mister Jack, Miss Gwenie, this is my best friend from North Fairwilde. She's going to visit us a while. Mister Fred called her last week and asked if she'd like to stay with us and look for work here." Bertille cut her eyes over at Priscilla, who had a laser-lock on Noble. "I think she's going to."

Mom threw up her hands. "The house will be full. That's the way I like it."

"I'll be moving out as soon as my apartment's finished," Noble said.

"But you won't go far." Mom smiled at him.

Bertille chuckled as she set a plate of brownies on the oak table. Then she turned and commenced setting down steaming coffee cups.

Noble pulled out a straight-backed chair for Priscilla, sat next to her, and popped a sweet treat in his mouth, licking his lips. All cleaned up, groomed, and well-dressed, he wasn't a bad-looking dude.

The rest of them joined the first two at the table.

"How can I ever thank you?" Noble gazed at Dad with misty eyes.

Dad nodded toward Gwenie and Jack. "I think you already have."

Growing to appreciate Noble after all the trouble he'd caused hadn't been easy, but it wasn't Jack's place to judge him. He kept reminding himself that Noble eventually had helped them escape. Jack gave him a gentle slap on his back. "You saved my future, maybe my life too. Just a few days ago I was aimlessly riding around in my new car. I knew I'd soon throw my clothes in a suitcase and head for college. Other than that I had little direction. Now, I know I want to get married and see Gwenie every day for the rest of my life. And Noble, you better be at the wedding. Thanks to you, she's safe and sound."

Dad held up his coffee cup, " Here. Here. A toast to the future."

The End.

Award-winning author Gail Pallotta's a wife, Mom, swimmer and bargain shopper who loves God, beach sunsets and getting together with friends and family. She's been a Sunday school teacher, a swim-team coordinator and an after-school literary instructor. A former regional writer of the year for American Christian Writers Association, she won Clash of the Titles in 2010. Her teen book, *Stopped Cold*, was a best-seller on All Romance eBooks, finished fourth in the Preditors and Editors readers' poll, and was a finalist for the 2013 Grace Awards. She's published short stories in "Splickety" magazine and *Sweet Freedom with a Slice of Peach Cobbler*. Some of her published articles appear in anthologies while two are in museums. Visit her web site at http://www.gailpallotta.com

Coming soon *Barely above Water* from Prism Book Group.

Made in the USA
Middletown, DE
17 August 2015